SECRETS OF THE
CASTLETON
MANOR LIBRARY™

Up to Noir Good

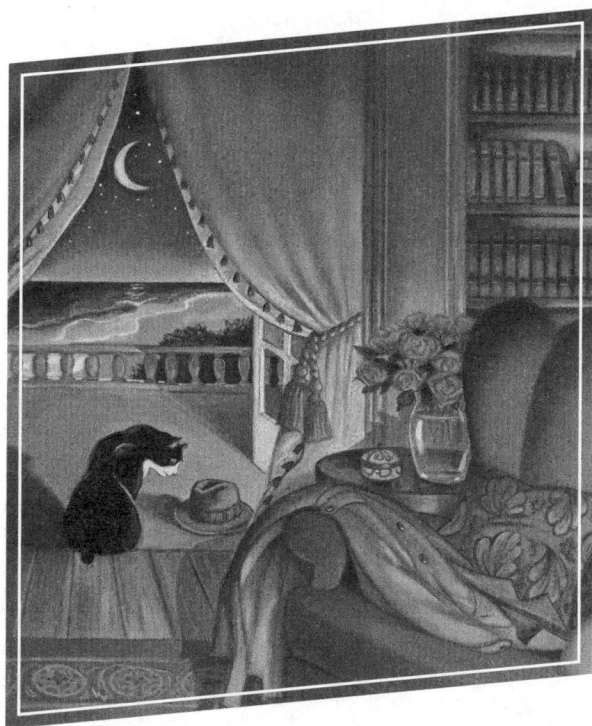

Jan Fields

Annie's®
AnniesFiction.com

Books in the Secrets of the Castleton Manor Library series

Library of Congress-in-Publication Data
Up to Noir Good/ by Jan Fields
p. cm.
I. Title
          2017964030

AnniesFiction.com
(800) 282-6643
Secrets of the Castleton Manor Library™
Series Creator: Shari Lohner
Series Editor: Lorie Jones
Cover Illustrator: Jesse Reisch

10 11 12 13 14 | Printed in China | 9 8 7 6 5

"Very few of us are what we seem."
—*Agatha Christie*

1

After the heat of an August day, the blast of cold from the water-side restaurant's air-conditioning was startling, and Faith Newberry shivered even while she appreciated the relief. She blinked and peered around Driftwood. Though not dark, the lights were dimmed to make the large room feel cooler.

"It's very . . . open," Faith said to her aunt. Her sun-dazzled vision hadn't quite recovered enough to determine much else.

"You're going to love it," Eileen Piper assured her, giving Faith's arm a light pat to coax her closer to the hostess stand. As usual, Eileen wore her medium-brown hair pulled back, out of her face. She turned her warm smile toward the hostess.

Wearing the nearly ubiquitous uniform of service—a crisp white shirt and a black skirt—the slender young woman with short dark hair smiled at them as they approached. Her shirt pocket was embroidered with a seagull perched on a twisted piece of driftwood. Faith had seen the same logo on the sign outside. "Welcome to Driftwood," the hostess said. "Two?"

"Yes," Eileen said. "We'd like to sit outside if there's a table open."

Outside? Faith gaped at her aunt for a moment, wondering what exactly about their sweltering walk across the parking lot made Eileen think they should eat outside. Eileen's pale pink blouse and Bermuda shorts looked cool, but Faith's own white knit top and pencil skirt had left her gasping from the heat when they had gotten out of her SUV. "Are you sure? It seems quite nice in here."

In truth, the details of the restaurant's interior were still a little shadowy from the light blindness, but she could tell the decor featured lots of blue hues and pale wood, and they hadn't gone in for an overabundance of fishing nets as was common in so many seafood restaurants. They also didn't crowd the tables together, which she appreciated as well.

"You'll like it." Eileen winked at Faith. "Trust me."

"Right this way, please." The hostess grabbed a couple of menus and guided them to the deck.

The outside tables were shaded by huge umbrellas, but Faith could see immediately that wasn't the main appeal of sitting on the deck. It was the view of the sparkling water beyond, dotted with brightly colored sailboats. A breeze blew in off the bay, making the deck substantially cooler than the parking lot had been.

The hostess ushered them to a table near the deck rail and set their menus down on it. After assuring them their server would be with them soon, she left.

Faith slid into a chair, and the shade from the umbrella cooled her skin, warmed from the short walk to the deck. "It's spectacular here," she said.

Eileen picked up her menu from the table. "I know you love the water, and the sailboats are always so bright and cheery." She turned toward the bay. "You should have Wolfe take you sailing sometime."

Faith stared at her aunt in surprise for the second time in five minutes, wondering if she might have gotten too much sun. "Wolfe Jaxon is my boss. I can't just up and ask him to take me sailing."

Eileen opened the menu but kept her gaze on Faith. "You underestimate yourself. You always have. So tell me what has you so grumpy."

Faith frowned. "I'm not grumpy."

Eileen shrugged and perused the menu. "Sure you're not."

Faith stared pointedly at her own menu, determined to change the subject and show that she was definitely *not* grumpy. "Do you eat here often? What do you like?"

Eileen set aside her menu. "Sadly, it would be an exaggeration to say I eat here often. But I try to get here every now and then. I recommend the crab cakes. They're wonderfully seasoned, and the crab is always fresh." The corner of her mouth quirked, and she fiddled with her napkin. "Plus, you can relate to crabs today."

"My aunt—full-time librarian, part-time comic," Faith said drily, but she couldn't hold back a grin at her aunt's twinkling blue eyes.

Eileen was the head librarian of the Candle House Library. Located in the historic downtown of Lighthouse Bay, the library was privately funded and hugely popular, though Faith suspected part of the popularity was directly connected to Eileen. Her aunt was one of the kindest people she knew, and her passion for literature was tangible.

Faith noticed Eileen watching her appraisingly. "Okay, I might be the teensiest bit crabby," she admitted. "I'll make an effort to be better company."

Before Eileen could respond, a waitress appeared and asked for their beverage orders. Eileen chose the peach tea and went ahead and ordered her crab cakes as well. Faith echoed her aunt's order, and the waitress bustled away.

"You don't have to be better company," Eileen said. "I'm perfectly happy with your company whether you're grumpy or not, but I would like to know what's bothering you."

Faith leaned back in her chair and watched a bright red sailboat drift by. "It's the upcoming literary retreat. I'm usually excited for each new event, but this one really isn't my cup of tea."

Also a librarian, Faith worked at Castleton Manor, where she curated the most amazing book collection she'd ever seen. The château-style mansion was a high-end, seaside haven for bibliophiles who wanted to slip away from the real world to indulge their love of books. Among her other duties, Faith also gave lectures for the guests on topics related to each retreat theme, and that was where her present problem came from.

Eileen raised her eyebrows. "A librarian who doesn't like a literary retreat? I'm all ears. What kind of retreat is it?"

"It's called So Noir, and it features hard-boiled detectives." Faith sighed. "I know you've never met a mystery you didn't like, but I've never cared for the genre. I find the worldview so bleak with the focus on the worst impulses of humanity. Everyone steals. Everyone cheats. Faithfulness is a myth. I simply can't enjoy that kind of outlook."

"Maybe reading about a world that is so much darker makes people feel better about their own circumstances," Eileen suggested. "Plus, the genre is larger than you might think. I especially enjoy some of the female noir writers like Sara Paretsky, Megan Abbott, and Margaret Millar, though her books are hard to find. I have more noir authors in our library collection."

"I have read the Dizzy Dame novels by Cass Morton," Faith admitted. "But they're so funny that I think calling them noir is a stretch."

"Writing a parody of a serious genre like noir is tough," Eileen said. "She does it well."

"She's going to give a speech during lunch at the retreat tomorrow. You should come."

"I'd love to," Eileen said, "if I can sneak away."

The waitress arrived and set sweating glasses of tea in front of Faith and her aunt. "Your food will be here directly."

As soon as the waitress walked away, Faith took a sip of her tea. "They're quite prompt here."

"Surprisingly so, considering the place is so popular," Eileen agreed. "But keep in mind that they can be a little optimistic when they talk about how soon the food is coming."

"Good point." Faith set her glass on a coaster that was shaped like a large seashell and gazed again toward the water. The sight of so much beauty did make her feel better. Of course, she was surrounded by beauty when she was at work. The Castleton library alone was breathtaking.

"The noir novels in my 'Mystery Loves Company' section are among the most popular books at the Candle House Library," Eileen said, pulling Faith's attention back to their conversation. "And I have a definite soft spot for Sam Spade."

"I should have asked you to come and do the presentation for the retreat. You're unquestionably more knowledgeable on the subject," Faith said. "I'm doing a talk on vintage noir books as collectibles, but I worry that the attendees will find the subject boring."

"I doubt anyone could find one of your talks boring, and people are always interested in the value of things they own," Eileen said. "Does the library have many noir novels in the collection?"

Faith nodded. "More than I would have expected. Dashiell Hammett and Raymond Chandler as well as lesser-known authors. We have several novels by James M. Cain and an anthology of the *Black Mask* magazine stories from various authors including Carroll John Daly."

Eileen smiled. "Maybe I should come and browse your collection sometime. I'd love to see that anthology."

"You'd be welcome, of course." Faith made a face. "Even if Marlene grumbles, Wolfe likes you, so you're safe."

"Is there anything Marlene doesn't grumble about?" her aunt asked.

Faith couldn't think of anything. Marlene Russell, the assistant manager of Castleton Manor, was a study in contrasts. She loved Castleton but hated the policy of allowing pets with their potential for disaster. She had an air of rigid toughness, but she loved Regency romances. She could also be the bane of Faith's existence—and that of every other Castleton Manor employee—though occasionally she showed moments of softening.

"Eileen!"

Faith and her aunt turned toward a tall blonde strolling across the boardwalk on astoundingly high heels. The woman wore her hair in an old-fashioned victory roll with a few short, tight curls over her face.

Eileen stood as the other woman approached. "Good afternoon, Louellyn."

Before Eileen could utter another word, Louellyn engulfed her in a hug. "You should tell me when you're coming in." She wagged a finger at Eileen. "I could have the chef make you something special. I have pull here," she added, laughing heartily.

"Oscar *is* making me something special," Eileen said. "Crab cakes. You know they're my favorite." Then she swept a hand toward Faith. "This is my niece Faith Newberry. She's the librarian at Castleton Manor. Faith, this is Louellyn North. She co-owns Driftwood and happens to be married to the chef, Oscar."

Faith stood to shake the tall woman's hand. Despite her height, everything about Louellyn seemed softly rounded, from the blonde curls and rolled hair to her wide eyes fringed with what had to be false eyelashes.

"Your aunt and I have known each other for many years," Louellyn said. "Her mama and mine were the best of friends when I was a tiny girl. Eileen was a wise teenager then. She had no choice but to put up with my adoration. We were constantly thrown together, and we had to make the best of it."

"You make it sound like a trial," Eileen said. "As I remember it, we had a great time."

Louellyn winked at Faith. "I got your aunt into so much mischief. When I was a little girl, I never saw trouble that I didn't like."

"And thankfully she still feels that way." A man who matched Louellyn's towering height smiled as he joined them. He had a hawk nose and blue eyes that were in stark contrast to the black curls on his head.

Louellyn laughed and held out her arm to him. "Oscar, come and meet Eileen's niece. She's a librarian too. She works at Castleton Manor." She grinned at Faith. "Eileen talks about you all the time."

"Only good things, I hope," Faith said.

"How could it be anything else?" Oscar boomed as he shook Faith's hand. "It is a pleasure to meet you. I certainly do not remember the librarians of my youth looking like you and your lovely aunt. They were all severe old women in my mind. Otherwise, I might have visited more often."

The women laughed.

"I read that Castleton Manor was hosting a So Noir retreat," Oscar remarked. "I belonged to that group long ago and went to one of their retreats. I loved it."

Faith smiled, glad he hadn't overheard her complaining earlier. "Some of the events at the So Noir retreat are open to the public if you'd like to call for tickets."

"I won't be able to attend." He turned a rueful glance toward his wife. "We must be careful with our money these days."

Louellyn frowned. "I would think we could afford a single event." She motioned to the filled tables. "We've been doing well."

Oscar's face darkened. "Castleton is not an inexpensive venue."

"The speaking events are quite reasonable," Faith assured him.

"I am sure they are," Oscar said, then waved a hand in the air. "But it is hard. You would be shocked at the expenses in such a place as this. We are like hamsters on a wheel, constantly running and never going anywhere."

From the cold expression on Louellyn's face, Faith suspected this was a sensitive topic, so she hastily changed the subject. "I'm really excited to taste the crab cakes that Eileen raved about."

"Then I must rush them along," Oscar said. "Can I speak with you in the kitchen, my love?"

"Of course," Louellyn said tightly. She smiled at Faith and Eileen and wished them a good day.

As they walked away, Faith raised an eyebrow at her aunt. "That was a little frosty."

"And odd. I suppose everyone has off days." Then she picked up her glass. Before taking a sip, she gave Faith another teasing look. "Even librarians."

After an absolutely decadent lunch, Faith dropped Eileen off at the Candle House Library and headed to work. She knew the guests would be checking in for the retreat, and Marlene wanted the library to be open for at least a few hours the first day, since the guests often liked to explore the magnificent space even before going to their rooms.

As she expected, she saw a few people pulling wheeled luggage into the lobby. Faith smiled as she thought of the pleasant surprise they had waiting for them upstairs. Castleton Manor had eighteen suites, most of them with their own fireplaces, though she doubted anyone would want to make use of that feature in the summer heat, even with the mansion's excellent air-conditioning. Each suite was named for a famous author, fictional character, or place. The suites were large and elaborately decorated to match the room's theme, including shelves of related books. For avid readers, it was like spending time away with beloved old friends.

When she let herself into the library, Faith was surprised to see Watson, her black-and-white tuxedo cat, staring at her through the tall French doors that led to the terrace.

With a groan, Faith quickly crossed the room and opened the door. "What are you doing out there, Rumpy?" she asked, using her pet name for him. She called him that because he was missing most of his tail due to an injury when he was a kitten. "I told you to stay in the cottage today."

Watson simply strolled by her with a twitch of his stump of a tail.

There was nothing wrong with Watson's hearing, but he often acted as if Faith's commands fell on deaf ears, particularly when she called him Rumpy. He also possessed an uncanny ability to slip out of any room she put him in. The combination of the two sometimes drove Faith to distraction. But she'd loved the handsome cat from the moment she'd found him shivering in the snow as a kitten, and he'd saved her life more than once, so she could definitely overlook his more mischievous habits.

A sharp voice behind Faith jerked her attention away from Watson. "I'm glad to see you've decided to join us."

Faith resisted the urge to roll her eyes as she turned to face Marlene Russell. As always, the assistant manager was perfectly turned out in a crisp linen skirt and a tailored blouse. Her wavy blonde hair was flawless, as if no strand dared fall out of place. The only disorderly element to Marlene's ensemble was the messy pile of papers she held.

"Actually I'm back thirty minutes early," Faith said calmly.

"That's good because I need you to take on an additional responsibility this evening." Marlene thrust the stack of loose papers at her. "The keynote speaker for opening night is in the hospital."

"Oh no. What happened?"

"He ate some bad oysters and has food poisoning. Fortunately, he didn't eat them here, but I believe we should avoid mentioning food poisoning at all. We'll simply say he was called away suddenly. We don't want to give guests the wrong idea."

"No, I'm sure not." Faith glanced down at the haphazard pile of papers and wondered what they had to do with her.

"Those are the speaker's notes," Marlene explained. "I need you to put together a speech about the detective's code. It's listed in the events, so you'll have to stick to that topic."

Faith stared at Marlene in horror. "I can't put together an opening-night speech in a couple of hours. This is one of the ticketed events. There's no telling how many people will be expecting to hear from an actual expert on noir."

"Of course you can do it," she huffed. "It's about a book genre, and you're a reasonably competent librarian. Besides, you have the man's notes. You'll be fine."

Faith leafed through the pile of handwritten pages. There was no order, no clear thread tying the pile of scribbles together. Some of the notes had even been written on a napkin. "I don't know where to begin."

"I have complete faith in you," Marlene said, though her tone sounded anything but supportive. "After all, you were hired because of your familiarity with a wide variety of literary topics."

As I remember, Faith thought, *you never wanted to hire me in the first place.* She shuffled the papers in her hands a little more but found no obvious answer to her problem within them. "I'll need to close the library so I can focus."

"Absolutely not," Marlene snapped. "You know the guests love this library and they'll want to come in and see it. They always do. If you need more help focusing, perhaps you could put that cat out." She scowled in Watson's direction. "He's a distraction if ever I saw one."

Before Faith could say something in Watson's defense, Marlene spun on her heel and sailed out of the library.

Watson jumped up onto the table beside Faith and pawed at the papers in her hand.

Faith stared forlornly at them. "Watson, I think I'm doomed."

2

Faith stood near the base of the statue of Dame Agatha Christie and gazed down the long two-story Great Hall Gallery. The elegant room was dotted with small tables draped in snow-white cloths. Dressed in crisp black and white, servers carrying trays of canapés and beverages wove between the tables and the chattering groups of guests.

At the moment, the gallery seemed to be rapidly filling with far more people than Faith had expected. Most of the time the audiences for her library talks were relatively small, but the keynote address was open to the public, so she knew that had swollen the attendance. It was obvious a number of people were taking the opportunity to visit Castleton, eat some high-end food, and listen to a hastily assembled speech that was surely going to result in booing and probably the end of a wonderful job. Faith put a hand to her chest, reminding herself that it wouldn't help the evening if she gave in to her imagination.

Faith realized she was fidgeting nervously with the delicate silver pendant on the chain around her neck, and she dropped her hands to her sides. Her notes were already on the speaker's podium nearby, but she wished she had them in her hands to go through again. She was overwhelmed at the thought of being unprepared in front of so many people.

She glanced up at the statue's serene face watching over the beautiful gallery room. *It's easy for you to be calm*, Faith thought. *You don't have to give a speech tonight.*

With a shiver, Faith fought the urge to wrap her arms around herself. She hadn't expected the air-conditioning to be quite this aggressive when she picked out the light silk-and-linen dress she wore.

The dress and low-heeled shoes had been perfect for the warm walk from her cottage to the manor.

As she scanned the audience, she understood the decision behind cranking up the air-conditioning. Trench coats were definitely the most common costume choice, which was only to be expected in a group fond of ace detectives.

Faith smiled slightly as she counted the number of fedoras perched on the heads of both the male and female guests. Some of the women had chosen to dress as the dame instead, and Faith spotted several platinum blondes with elaborately styled hair. Around the room, she noticed a smattering of small dogs in laps, a few with little fedoras of their own.

Then she caught sight of a familiar friendly face. Wolfe Jaxon, co-owner of Castleton Manor, stood near the stairs. As always, Wolfe was easily the most handsome man in the room with his tall, athletic build, at least as far as Faith was concerned. His thick, dark hair streaked with gray and his clear blue eyes certainly didn't hurt.

When their gazes met, Wolfe smiled and nodded at her, raising a glass of champagne.

Faith smiled back, but it felt tight on her face.

Wolfe must have noticed her tension because he began to cross the room, heading straight for her.

She wasn't sure if she found that comforting or more stressful. She appreciated his desire to be supportive, but the thought that he was going to watch her crash and burn in front of all these people wasn't calming her nerves at all.

Wolfe's long stride closed the distance quickly. Since it was the first night of the event, most of the guests didn't yet know their host, so he wasn't stopped along the way. He set his champagne glass on a tray he passed on the way to Faith.

"You're looking terrified," he said quietly. "The guests are going to worry that we abuse you terribly here."

"I'm feeling terrified," Faith confessed. "I only got the notes for this speech a couple of hours ago, and they weren't entirely coherent. I'm beginning to suspect the original speaker isn't really sick. He's hiding under a bed somewhere."

Wolfe nodded. "I heard about the sudden replacement. If this is too much for you, just tell me. I can speak to everyone in your place." He smiled enough to show a flash of dimple in his cheek. "I *have* read a detective novel or two."

As much as Faith would have loved handing the job off to someone else, she hated to admit defeat now. Besides, she had no doubt that Marlene would find a dozen ways to make her life miserable for not following her orders. "Thank you for the offer, but I think I can handle it."

"What's the speech about?" Wolfe asked.

Faith looked at him in surprise.

"I have to admit, I've been so busy with my other work that I haven't done much more than sign off on things. I know the retreat has a noir theme, but otherwise, I'm a bit in the dark. Marlene has more than earned her keep with this one."

"I'll be talking about the detective's code," she said.

"Ah, 'When a man's partner is killed he's supposed to do something about it,'" Wolfe said, quoting Sam Spade in *The Maltese Falcon*. "I actually like the idea of a code. We all need to draw lines in the sand for ourselves. A few times I've had to make decisions about the right way versus the easy way."

"No doubt you'd have made a fine private eye yourself," Faith said. "Though I dislike the whole cynical view of the world as corrupt with only a few standing in the way of that corruption." She gestured to the statue of Agatha Christie. "I prefer cozy mysteries where most people are good."

"But even Agatha Christie novels are written with the belief that you cannot truly know what goes on inside other people," he reasoned. "Even the mildest of appearances can contain darkness within."

"I suppose that's true," Faith conceded. "But I'd feel safer in St. Mary Mead than the cities in any of the noir novels."

"That is a key difference," Wolfe said. "The city is an important part of noir. Lew Archer would be lost in St. Mary Mead or Lighthouse Bay."

"Though we seem to have a roomful of them tonight." She glanced at the guests. "Either that or there was an amazing sale on trench coats."

Wolfe chuckled. "And matching fedoras."

"Not always *matching*."

Wolfe chuckled again.

Faith found the sound of his laughter went a long way toward making her feel better, but then her churning stomach knotted anew when Marlene walked away from one group of guests and headed for the podium.

She tapped the microphone on the podium, and a soft thumping rang out.

At that, most of the standing guests scurried to find seats.

Faith laced her fingers together to still the shaking in her hands, wincing at how clammy they felt.

Wolfe gave her an encouraging smile, and she appreciated his support.

"Good evening," Marlene said, offering the guests a practiced smile. "And welcome to the first day of the So Noir retreat."

The group applauded politely.

Then the assistant manager droned on with various announcements for the retreat.

Faith's mind drifted to a dream she used to have in college where she'd be in front of a class, giving a speech on a topic she knew nothing about. In the dream, she'd fumble with her notes and discover they were written in a foreign language that she couldn't read. She sincerely hoped her real-life version was going to turn out better than the one in the dream, which usually ended with booing and fruit throwing. She snuck a glance at one of the trays of canapés. Thankfully, they looked too light to be thrown.

She was reminded of the advice to picture the audience in their underwear, something that usually made her feel more embarrassed than relaxed.

Considering how many people in the crowd were wearing some combination of trench coat and fedora, precious few of them reminded her of Humphrey Bogart in *The Maltese Falcon*, which was what she suspected they were shooting for. There were guests who appeared to be in their twenties, and others who clutched canes and had snow-white hair under their fedoras.

One unlikely pair caught her attention—a tall, whip-thin blonde clutching a small terrier in her arms stood close to a shorter, bald man who held his fedora in his hand and mopped his brow with a handkerchief.

Then she noticed that about half of the attendees were clearly ignoring Marlene in favor of glazed stares at their cell phones.

How do I even get the attention of these people?

Faith jumped slightly when she heard Marlene say her name.

The assistant manager turned away from the podium and made a sweeping gesture as if welcoming Faith, though Marlene's intense expression was anything but welcoming.

"Good luck," Wolfe whispered, giving her the slightest push. "You're going to be great."

Walking to the podium, Faith pasted a smile on her face and let her gaze sweep the audience. "Thank you, Ms. Russell," she said, nodding politely at Marlene.

Gathering her notes from the lower shelf of the podium, Faith used the movement to take one more deep, calming breath. Then she lined up the notes on top of the podium and scanned the audience again.

Two men slouched in their chairs with their arms crossed. They scowled at her.

Faith reminded herself that they might be trying to appear tough and not really be so difficult to impress.

Then she saw a matronly woman in a pink fedora and trench coat who held an adorable Maltese in a matching pink hat.

The woman smiled brightly at Faith. She was clearly eager for the opening talk.

At the woman's warm welcome, Faith felt herself loosen up. "As most of you know, the detective's code drives the life of the noir antihero," she began. "It doesn't always align with the law or the ethics of those around him."

As she spoke, Faith recognized one of the people in the audience. Louellyn North made her way through the tables to reach one of the few empty ones not far from the podium. To her surprise, Faith noticed a man following Louellyn. *That's not Oscar North.* Like most of the audience, the man wore a trench coat with the collar turned up, but Louellyn had chosen to go with the femme fatale look, wearing a rather racy red dress.

Louellyn ignored the man when he pulled out a chair at the table for her. Instead, she strode past him and slipped into the opposite seat without his assistance.

Whoever he is, Faith thought, *he likes her more than she likes him.*

Though Faith kept as much of her attention as possible on her notes, she found herself distracted by the drama playing out before her. The man seemed to be trying to hold Louellyn's attention while she virtually ignored him.

At one point, Louellyn made eye contact with Faith and smiled, wiggling her fingers in greeting.

Faith gave the woman a slight nod in return.

As Faith continued her talk, she let her gaze roam the audience, but her attention returned to Louellyn often. She noticed the tall woman glancing frequently toward the back of the room. Faith assumed she must be watching for her husband, and she wondered if Oscar would be joining his wife. She hoped so since it seemed to be important to Louellyn.

When her split attention made her stumble over the name of one of the noir authors, Faith gave herself a mental shake. She pushed down her natural curiosity over the restaurant owners and focused on the detective's code.

She was distracted only once more when she spotted a flash of black and white near a tall urn filled with greenery that stood along one wall. Faith paused and took a sip of water to cover as she peered at the planter. As she expected, she saw Watson hop up onto the edge of the urn and begin to nonchalantly wash his face.

Don't do anything to get Marlene's attention, she begged silently, wishing she had a way to get the cat out of the room.

The cat noticed his human looking at him, so he pointedly turned his back on her. He couldn't have her thinking he was moved by her annoyance. She was always scolding him for one thing or another. As a cat, he was above all that.

His whiskers twitched as he smelled something fishy. He was fairly certain one of the trays that had just passed by in the hands of a strange human male contained something delicious, but he would have to consider how to get some. The human was too far away for even a skilled jumper to reach.

The cat turned again, putting his back to the enticing scent in a forced display of disinterest. It probably wasn't very good anyway. Humans were always putting dreadful items like lemons or pepper on top of their fish. Why did they insist on eating things that could make a cat sneeze? Sneezing was so undignified.

With his face pointed back toward his human, he deigned to listen to her for a moment.

"*The hard-boiled detective is driven by curiosity,*" she explained, "*constantly pulling any string he finds to unravel the case.*"

The cat was surprised to find his human actually talking about something interesting. He wasn't sure why anyone would want to boil a detective, but he could definitely relate to anyone who enjoyed pulling strings. He was soon listening so intently he forgot about washing and sat like a statue with his paw in midair.

As his human continued to speak, the code she described sounded familiar. It seemed these detectives were smart and tough, two rather catlike qualities.

Plus, they spent much of their time saving hapless humans. He could relate to that as well. His human constantly put herself into dangerous situations. She would be completely lost without him.

The cat sat up tall, holding his head high, as he realized exactly what was going on. His human was talking about him! She finally understood that he was a true hero, even if she was rather confusing on the issue of being boiled. He hoped she wasn't suggesting some kind of hot bath for him, because he would quickly dissuade her of that idea. Cats preferred to do their own bathing. Like those detectives, cats lived life on their own terms.

At last, the humans around him indulged in the ridiculous habit of banging their hands together.

He knew from experience that this irritating display was in fact a signal for his human to step away from the podium, where she could pay better attention to him.

Taking a deep breath, the cat prepared to launch into a good yowl so she'd know the importance of coming straight over and possibly getting him some of those little fishy bits.

But before the cat could even open his mouth, the doors to the library flew open.

A strange human staggered through the door, shouting.

Everyone at the tables jumped to their feet, wailing in distress.

The words the stranger had shouted penetrated the cat's awareness, which had been momentarily distracted by the bedlam around him. A dead body?

That could mean only one thing.

His next case!

3

Marlene rushed to the microphone and practically shoved Faith out of the way while Wolfe caught the arm of the panicked witness and walked with him into the library.

"Please remain in your seats," Marlene ordered in a firm voice.

The guests paid Marlene no attention. Obviously a group of detective-novel enthusiasts were not about to stay in the gallery when there was a dead body nearby. There was simply no stopping the stampede. Marlene and Faith were swept along in the tide.

Faith searched for Wolfe, but she didn't spot him until they were out on the tiled terrace outside the library.

On one side of the terrace, not far from the ornate stone railing, Wolfe knelt next to a man's body sprawled on the tiles and pressed his fingers to the man's neck. From the troubled expression on Wolfe's face, she could tell he wasn't finding a pulse.

"Please stand back," Faith called out as she edged through the group. "The police are on their way." She didn't know if they were. Should she have called them? She exchanged glances with Wolfe, and he nodded. The police had been called.

Wolfe stood and positioned himself between the body and the crowd. He held up both hands. "Stand back. We do not want to destroy any evidence. As mystery fans, I'm sure you understand."

The crowd seemed more inclined to listen to Wolfe or more doubtful of their ability to get past him as they stopped pushing and stood a few feet from the body, talking amongst themselves.

Faith was glad to leave crowd control to Wolfe, but she saw Marlene muscle through the group to stand beside the body, giving the crowd her fiercest glare.

From where she stood, Faith could see only the dead man's back and a small bit of the back of his head. That was fine with her. She had seen enough dead bodies. Despite the heat of the summer evening, she felt chilled and hugged herself.

Something warm and fuzzy brushed against her ankle, and she jumped. She spotted Watson slinking toward the sprawled victim. She stepped forward to grab the cat, but he must have sensed her coming after him because he tensed his muscles and sprang.

Faith caught him in the middle of a leap that would have landed him on top of the poor man. "Watson," she scolded under her breath, "cut it out."

Faith was now close enough to see the victim, and she gasped when she recognized him. It was Oscar North. She could see no obvious cause of death, but she did notice that he wasn't wearing the trench coat that was favored by so many people in the audience. Instead, he wore a white sport coat.

Faith twisted around to scan the crowd. Did Louellyn know about her husband? If not, maybe Faith could prevent her from learning this way. Then she heard a scream. She hadn't moved fast enough.

The crowd opened up around Louellyn, who stood with her hands pressed to her deathly pale face.

Faith hurried to the woman's side. "Louellyn? It's Faith. Eileen's niece. Let me get you inside."

Louellyn stared at Faith, wide-eyed. "That's Oscar. Why isn't anyone helping him?" She tried to push past Faith. "Get out of my way! I need to help him. I need to help my husband."

Wolfe swiftly put himself between Louellyn and the body. "I'm sorry, but you can't help him. Please let Faith take you inside. We'll come get you if anything changes."

Louellyn tried to peer around Wolfe, but he kept himself between her and Oscar, speaking in his calm, warm voice the whole time. Finally, she stopped moving and simply stood still, staring into Wolfe's face almost without expression.

"Please go with Faith," he insisted, his voice firm but not unkind.

She nodded, and Faith led her into the library. Louellyn must have passed through the library with the rest of the mob, but it was clear that she was seeing it now for the first time. She stumbled when she glanced up at the towering ceiling of the two-story room.

The manor's library was truly magnificent and housed more books than many public libraries. The carved walnut ceiling that soared overhead matched similarly carved walnut furniture throughout the room. With the towering built-in bookcases that held thousands of volumes, the room never failed to fill Faith with awe, but after gaping at the ceiling, Louellyn seemed not to notice the grandeur around her. Faith couldn't blame her.

Faith's destination was a large fireplace where a grouping of red velvet chairs and settees offered comfortable seating for any guest who wanted to read in the opulent room. She led Louellyn to one of the chairs across from the fireplace that didn't provide a direct view of the terrace. Since it was a warm night and there was no event planned for inside the library, the fireplace grate was empty. Louellyn gazed into it just the same, though her blank expression suggested she didn't actually see it.

Faith sat in the chair beside Louellyn, speaking quietly. Later she couldn't have repeated exactly what she said, only knowing she was trying for a quiet, comforting tone.

Watson seemed to appear out of nowhere and leaped into the distraught woman's lap.

Horrified, Faith hopped up to shoo the cat away, but Louellyn wrapped her arms around Watson and leaned her face against his head. He purred loudly. Since it was obvious Watson was helping Louellyn more than Faith had been, she left him alone and returned to her chair.

While Louellyn cuddled Watson, Faith took a moment to think about her brief glimpse of Oscar North's body. She wondered if the man might have suffered a heart attack. He'd seemed like an emotional person when she met him. As sad as any loss was, Faith hoped Oscar's passing was from natural causes.

Louellyn loosened her hold on Watson and settled for stroking him while staring into the empty fireplace again. Faith noticed that a faint color had returned to the woman's face.

"Did you know Oscar was here at the manor?" Faith asked gently. "I remember he'd said earlier that he wouldn't be coming."

Louellyn pulled her attention away from the fireplace with visible effort. She regarded Faith for a moment, then spoke in a hoarse voice. "He said he wouldn't come, but I hoped he would change his mind. I thought it would be good for him to get away from the restaurant for the evening." At that her eyes flooded with the first tears Faith had seen from her. Obviously the shock of her husband's death was sinking in enough for her to begin processing it as reality.

Faith didn't say anything as she waited for her to continue.

"That last thing I said to him was so ugly. I was tired of him working all the time, but I wish I hadn't left after speaking so angrily."

"Perhaps Oscar meant to surprise you by coming tonight," Faith suggested. "The fact that he was here surely shows that he had forgiven you."

Louellyn nodded. "But why was he on the terrace? He knew the event was inside. I had to come through the foyer to pick up my ticket. Why would he be on the terrace?" She looked intently at Faith as if she expected an answer. "It doesn't make sense."

"I don't know," Faith said softly. "May I ask who you were sitting with? I saw a man at your table earlier, and he seemed to know you, but I didn't see him with you outside."

"Sitting with?" Louellyn echoed as if the question confused her.

Faith wondered if Louellyn might be in shock. She wasn't sure what one did for physiological shock. She remembered in the past when she'd experienced a shocking event and someone gave her hot chocolate or something else sweet. That seemed to help. Should she get Louellyn some hot chocolate?

"Oh, that was Preston," Louellyn said finally, pulling Faith out of her fretting. "He's our business partner at Driftwood. I didn't expect to see him here. I'd forgotten he was a noir fan like Oscar." Her expression turned stricken as soon as she spoke her husband's name. She leaned toward Faith. "Who could have killed him?"

Faith raised a hand. "We don't know that anyone killed him. I didn't see any sign of injury." Though she had also avoided looking too closely at the body. "Perhaps he just collapsed."

"He wasn't that old!" Louellyn wailed before making a visible effort to get herself under control.

"Age isn't always a factor," Faith said. "Sometimes health issues hide. And Oscar seemed like a hard worker."

Louellyn's eyes widened. "He was working so hard. He almost never missed a dinner at the restaurant." She shook her head slowly. "What will I do without him?"

Faith certainly didn't have an answer, but she also didn't have an answer to where Louellyn's business partner had gone. Wouldn't he have wanted to be with Louellyn when she was in such dire need of emotional support?

"Let me see if I can get you something to drink," Faith said. "Would you like a glass of water? Or maybe hot chocolate?"

Louellyn blinked a few times. "Hot chocolate in the middle of summer?"

"I thought it might be calming."

The woman shook her head. "That's a winter drink to me. A glass of water would be nice."

"I'll be right back with it. And maybe some tea."

Louellyn nodded absently.

Faith left Louellyn petting Watson and staring into the fireplace. She walked out of the library and into the gallery, then crossed to a side table where a pitcher of ice water and glasses sat for just that purpose. The huge gallery was empty of guests, though a few manor employees scurried around gathering used glasses and plates from the tables.

Faith approached the nearest employee. "Could you please go down to the kitchen and have someone bring a cup of hot tea to the library? It's for the wife of the man who died."

"Of course," the young man said, then turned and darted across the room, heading for the stairs.

Faith returned to the side table and poured a glass of water for Louellyn. As she carried it back into the library, she noticed the crowd still milling around on the terrace. Thankfully, the press of gawkers in trench coats meant she couldn't see Oscar's body.

Swallowing down her own horror at the events of the evening, Faith offered the glass to Louellyn.

The woman's hand trembled as she took the glass. "Thank you. You've been so kind."

"Anyone would be," Faith said. "You've had a horrible shock."

Louellyn shook her head before taking a long sip of the cold water. "Not anyone. Some people can be cruel."

Faith wondered if Louellyn had someone specific in mind, but she didn't feel right grilling the grieving woman. "It's been my experience that people act out of the pain they're in."

"I suppose so."

A drop of water slid down the side of Louellyn's glass and landed right on Watson's head. If there was one absolute way to offend the cat, it was getting him wet. He shook his head and hopped down from her lap, then planted himself in front of the cold fireplace and started grooming himself.

"I've annoyed your cat," Louellyn said with a slight smile.

"Being a cat, he lives much of his life annoyed," Faith replied.

Watson refused to dignify any of that with a response.

Louellyn finished her water and set the glass down on the end table.

Faith was relieved to see that the woman's hand barely trembled anymore. Louellyn was definitely calming down. "Is there someone I can call for you?" she asked. "Maybe I could track down Preston."

Louellyn wrinkled her nose. "No thank you. I don't really know who I would call. I don't have family around here. And Oscar and I kept so busy at the restaurant that I didn't have much time to socialize."

"Owning a business must be challenging."

"It can be. Restaurants especially. Driftwood is always busy, but that's not enough."

"It's not?" Even though Faith recalled how Oscar had mentioned the restaurant's expenses, she was still surprised. The prices at Driftwood seemed in line with an upscale place. If it was always busy, why would there be financial problems?

"Apparently not." Louellyn laughed without humor. "I don't really know. I honestly think Oscar just says that so he'll have an excuse to do everything himself. He's a bit of a control freak." Then she froze and whispered, "Was. I guess it's *was* now, isn't it?"

Faith reached out to rest a hand on Louellyn's arm. "I'm so sorry."

Louellyn brushed away her tears. "I should get used to hearing that now. Everyone is going to be sorry. Do you really think Oscar worked himself to death? I should have made him take nights off. I should have insisted."

"Whatever happened, you can't blame yourself."

Louellyn laughed again. "Can't I? Isn't that what people do?"

It was then that the library doors opened and a small cart rolled in, pushed by Brooke Milner, the sous-chef at the manor and Faith's good friend. Brooke looked tired, but she smiled warmly at them. "I heard that you needed a cup of tea. I brought enough for both of you."

Louellyn seemed to welcome the distraction of answering questions about how she liked her tea as Brooke poured it. It was a true pot of tea, not simply tea bags.

Count on Brooke to pull out all the stops when someone needs comfort, Faith thought affectionately.

"This is a blueberry white tea," Brooke said, her tone even and soothing. "It is milder than a black tea, and the blueberry adds a nice, fresh flavor. I think you'll enjoy it."

When she handed over the cup, Louellyn raised it to her nose and inhaled deeply. "It smells wonderful. Thank you."

"We're happy to help with whatever you need," Brooke said. "I brought up some tea biscuits and a few finger sandwiches too. Shock can take a lot out of your body. Food helps."

"I don't think I could eat anything right now, but the tea is perfect." Louellyn settled back with her cup of tea, her hands wrapped around the china as if needing the warmth the cup provided.

Brooke shot a glance at Faith, curiosity sparkling in her eyes. Faith was sure she'd be thoroughly quizzed by her friend later, but Brooke merely said, "I'll leave the cart and send someone for it later. Faith knows how to contact me if you need anything else."

"Thank you, Brooke," Faith said. She walked Brooke to the door, then turned toward the French doors leading to the terrace. Now she saw the flash of a uniform she recognized. The Lighthouse Bay police had arrived.

Watson strolled over to stare out the French doors.

Faith was glad they were closed. The cat didn't need to be out on the terrace where he could potentially compromise the evidence. She'd never hear the end of it from the police—or Marlene, for that matter.

And Watson didn't need to be outside where he might be stepped on by one of the guests still wandering around on the terrace. Faith was a little surprised that so many guests remained outside. She would have expected Wolfe and Marlene to dispatch them sooner. She assumed the police would handle it now. Once everyone heard that Oscar's death was natural, the crime novel enthusiasts were sure to lose interest and head up to their rooms, especially considering some of the day's heat still radiated from the tiled terrace.

One of the French doors opened, and Faith started across the room with a cry of alarm. She knew she'd never reach the door in time to catch the cat.

To her surprise, a foot gently nudged Watson away from the door before Wolfe slipped through. He scooped up the cat and walked over to Faith with Watson in his arms.

The cat gave an annoyed meow, but he didn't resist being carried.

Wolfe handed Watson to Faith with a small smile as he passed her, then continued on to Louellyn. "Mrs. North, I wonder if the manor could offer you a ride home. Obviously you shouldn't be driving."

"I couldn't drive anyway. I took a taxi so I could ride home with Oscar." Louellyn managed a watery smile. "I hoped he would come, and now I wish he hadn't. I wish he was safe at home, waiting for me."

"Perhaps Preston would give you a lift," Faith suggested, scratching Watson under the chin. "Should I go find him?" His earlier behavior toward Louellyn had been so attentive that surely he would be willing to take her home. But that left Faith with the question of why he was absent now. Then she pushed the suspicious thought out of her head. Her idle speculation was inappropriate after what had happened. The poor woman's husband had taken ill and died.

"I don't know where he went, and I have no interest in hearing what he has to say about Oscar." Louellyn seemed shaken after speaking her husband's name, and the next thing she said came out slightly choked: "Shouldn't I stay with Oscar?"

"An ambulance is on the way to collect your husband," Wolfe said gently. "You will, of course, have decisions to make, but I believe they can wait until morning."

Louellyn stood and set her teacup on the rolling cart. "Then I would appreciate a ride home. I will have to call Oscar's brother." Her eyes swam with tears again. "How do I tell him about this? I don't even know what's going on."

"There's no script for this sort of thing," Wolfe said. "But you really shouldn't be alone. Are you sure we can't contact your friend?

Or perhaps a family member? Will your brother-in-law come over when you call?"

"No, he lives in California. There's no one, but I'll be all right."

Even after scolding herself for her curiosity, Faith couldn't help but wonder again where Oscar's business partner was. Then she realized she was overlooking the obvious solution. "Would you like me to call Eileen? I'm sure she would come and stay with you."

For a moment Faith thought Louellyn would agree, but she declined the offer. "I need to make some calls tonight, and then I think I'd rather be alone."

"If you change your mind, don't hesitate to call her," Faith said. "I know my aunt, and she'd come in an instant for a friend in need."

"You're so kind." Louellyn sighed deeply. "But the only need I have is for Oscar, and that's something no one can give me now."

"I'm afraid not," Faith said.

Louellyn's expression tightened. "Then I hope the police figure out who hurt my husband."

"We don't know that anyone hurt your husband," Wolfe said. "He could have taken ill or had an accident."

Louellyn shook her head. "Someone killed Oscar. And that person is going to pay."

4

The next morning, Faith still felt a little foggy as she peered at the most recent window display in the manor's gift and coffee shop. A statue, obviously intended to represent the one in *The Maltese Falcon*, stood in the center of the display next to a spill of coffee beans and packets of the house blend. Next to the bird, an upended fedora held different souvenirs.

The display was cute, but the sight of the fedora reminded Faith of the sea of fedoras in the audience the night before, which brought to mind the rest of the evening.

Iris Alden, the manager of the shop, called to her from behind the counter, "Are you going to come in or just admire the window all morning?"

A retired museum conservator who'd specialized in caring for early American art, Iris hadn't been able to handle having so much time on her hands after retirement, and she had come to work at Castleton Manor. Iris clearly thrived in her low-stress job at the gift shop. Faith had grown quite fond of her and her excellent coffee.

Faith walked into the shop. "It's lovely, but a cup of coffee would be even lovelier at the moment."

"Coming up." Iris turned to the coffeepot and poured a tall cup. "But I have to warn you. Marlene hasn't been in yet today, so you might not want to linger."

Faith knew that Marlene made a habit of stopping by the shop in the mornings to fine-tune the displays, which annoyed Iris to no end. "Thanks for the warning."

Iris handed over the cup of coffee. "I heard the retreat opening ceremonies didn't go quite as planned, though I also heard that you did a wonderful job with your talk."

"I'm sure my talk is not exactly the focal point of conversation right now."

"That poor man."

Faith took a sip of the hot coffee and sighed. "Yes, it was horrible. I'd actually met him and his wife yesterday afternoon."

"Now that's a spooky coincidence," Iris said.

"He didn't seem sick at all when I met him, but I suppose you never know."

Iris groaned. "Marlene is going to be unbearable after dealing with that tragedy last night. You know how much she hates it when the police come to Castleton." She glanced around the shop. "She'll be eager for someone to take it out on, and she'll end up redoing my displays."

"Maybe she'll be too busy this morning to come in," Faith said.

Iris appeared hopeful for a moment, then shook her head. "She gets twice as bad when she has to deal with complaints."

"Complaints? It's hardly Marlene's fault that the poor man collapsed."

"Guests don't always care if the complaint is logical."

Faith took another deep sip of coffee. "True, but I don't think there will be many complaints. The group was fairly excited when they rushed out to the terrace to stare at a dead body. It was positively ghoulish."

"Glad I missed it."

Faith let her gaze drift over the selection of pet treats in one of the displays. She wondered if she should buy some for Watson to make up for leaving him at the cottage. He never liked being left behind, but Faith knew guests would have questions about Oscar's death, and she didn't want to deal with those questions *and* Watson's rather impetuous nature.

Iris noticed where Faith was looking. "You just missed Midge. She restocked my pet treats after the initial run that always happens at the beginning of a new retreat."

Faith's friend Midge Foster owned Happy Tails Gourmet Bakery in town and was the concierge vet for the manor as well.

"I see she brought plenty of tunaroons," Faith said. "I'll take a few of them."

Iris grinned as she opened the display case. "Buying Watson's favorite treat. Are you feeling guilty about something?"

"I had to leave him behind at the cottage this morning. He hates that."

Iris laughed and handed over the bag of treats. "Good luck with his actually staying there."

Faith joined in the laugh, though hers was more than a little rueful. She wished she knew how Watson managed his spectacular escapes. Catching sight of the clock on the wall, she yelped. "Now I absolutely have to dash and open the library before the guests start lining up. See you later."

"Have a good day."

As always, the magnificence of Castleton Manor struck Faith afresh as she hurried through the halls toward the library. Where there was wood, it glowed with age and daily attention. Stone played an important part in the decor as well, including every possible shade of marble. And the expansive gardens meant that around every corner, guests could expect to see gorgeous arrangements bringing color and life to every nook and cranny.

Once she got to the library, Faith was surprised to see her prediction had not come true. None of the guests stood waiting by the library door, so she bustled around, straightening up and putting away a few stray books from the night before.

When the guests on the outside terrace had finally wandered in, they had been too wired to head straight up to their rooms. So they'd done what literary guests love best—they'd browsed the library, leaving it in a bit of a mess, which she'd been too tired to handle at that hour.

As Faith carefully reorganized the display of some of the most popular noir novels, her thoughts drifted to Louellyn. Faith wondered if she should call the poor woman to see how she was doing. On one hand, she barely knew Louellyn, having only met her the day before. She wasn't sure a call from her would be appreciated or appropriate. On the other hand, she *had* sat with her during what had to have been one of the toughest times of her life.

She decided to call her aunt. Eileen could check on Louellyn, and it wouldn't be intrusive since they were old friends.

Faith paused with a book in her hands as she realized she should have called Eileen last night when she'd gotten back to the cottage. Her aunt would want to know what had happened. In fact, Eileen might have wanted to check on Louellyn right away.

With a sigh, Faith slipped a hand into the pocket of the light jacket she'd chosen to wear inside the manor since the air-conditioning continued to be rather aggressive for her tastes. She started to pull out her phone, then dropped it back into her pocket when she heard the library door open.

Faith turned. To her surprise, the woman coming through the library doors wasn't a guest. It was Louellyn. She was followed by a stumpy-tailed black-and-white cat. Clearly Watson had not stayed at home where she'd left him.

She gave the cat a quick frown before crossing the room to Louellyn.

Louellyn burst into tears. "You have to help me," she gasped between sobs.

Faith led her to the chairs near the fireplace. "Of course. What do you need?"

Louellyn couldn't answer for several moments as she sobbed. Watson hopped up into her lap again, but even his calming presence didn't soothe her right away.

Faith hurried to bring her a box of tissues, then took the chair next to Louellyn and waited for the woman to regain control of herself.

Louellyn finally managed to speak. "The police came to my house," she said, her voice hoarse. "They think I killed Oscar."

"Killed?" Faith said. "They believe Oscar was murdered?"

Louellyn nodded as she burst into fresh sobs.

Watson shifted position on her lap, obviously uncomfortable with all the noise and the tears falling on his fur, but he didn't jump down. Faith wondered if he sensed how much Louellyn needed the company.

With a hiccup, Louellyn began speaking again. "I hope you'll help me."

"I'm not sure what you want me to do."

"I've heard about you," Louellyn said, her expression anxious. "Eileen told me you're clever at figuring things out. She said you've helped the police solve a number of crimes."

Faith didn't know what to say. She wasn't entirely sure the police had ever truly needed her assistance. Mostly she'd ended up in the middle of things and muddled her way through. Surely Louellyn wasn't confusing that with being some kind of detective. *Eileen, what have you gotten me into?*

"You have to help me," Louellyn insisted. "I'm desperate."

"The police in Lighthouse Bay are very good," Faith said gently. "I'm sure they'll find the truth. They're not in the habit of putting innocent people in jail." Then she winced. That wasn't completely true, but it certainly wasn't their habit. And she did have complete faith in Chief Andy Garris to sort things out in the end.

"You don't understand!" Louellyn wailed. "The chief of police practically accused me to my face."

"Do you have any idea why anyone would even suspect you?"

"I'm the wife," Louellyn said with a sniff. "Isn't that what they say on television? The police always suspect the spouse?"

"I don't think it's that automatic," Faith said.

"Well, we did have a fight." Louellyn glanced down at Watson and gave him an awkward pat on the head.

The cat gave Louellyn a look that Faith could only interpret as disgusted. Watson was particular about petting, and evidently Louellyn had gone too far. He hopped down onto the floor.

"What did you fight about?" Faith asked.

Louellyn brushed at the cat hair in her lap. "Money." She sighed. "It's always been about money lately. We've been fighting all the time. I hated that. I hate that the last thing Oscar and I did together was fight, but I didn't kill him. I love my husband."

"Were your financial affairs really so dire?"

Louellyn shrugged. "Apparently. Oscar had been acting weird about money lately. The restaurant was full every night and nearly every lunch, but he kept telling me I needed to spend less. I honestly don't spend that much."

"Of course," Faith said, though she recognized the purse hanging from Louellyn's shoulder and the shoes she was wearing. They were by designers that were well beyond Faith's budget. If Louellyn's closet was full of things like that, Faith could understand where financial problems might originate.

Dabbing her eyes again with the wad of tissues, Louellyn explained, "The latest row was about the tickets I bought for the opening-night event here. I thought it would be a nice surprise. Oscar loved that whole genre. He has a movie poster from *Chinatown* in his office at the restaurant. All the noir stuff was really Oscar's obsession, not mine. Though I did love Oscar's joy in it."

Faith wished she had something comforting to say, something profound. "It's good that you two could share that," she managed weakly.

Louellyn smiled sadly. "Whenever he saw me while we were first dating, he used to quote a line from *Casablanca*: 'Of all the gin joints in all the towns in all the world, she walks into mine.' Back then he always made me laugh with his silliness. He loved talking about *Casablanca*. He said it was a stew of all the movie genres but it did noir the best." She gazed up at Faith with her eyes full of tears. "How could anyone think I killed Oscar?"

"They don't know you," Faith said softly. *And neither do I.* "Since you'd already bought the tickets for opening night, I'm surprised Oscar didn't come with you."

"I was too. I even called in the chef we use on the few occasions Oscar is willing to let someone cover for him. I had it all settled. But then Oscar and I had that fight, and I stormed out. I came here to take my mind off the argument. I'd already paid for my ticket. If I didn't use at least one of the two, then I really would be wasting money like he accused me of doing. When I picked up my ticket in the foyer, I told them to hold the second one for Oscar. I kept watching for him. I was sure he'd walk in." With that, her composure broke again, and she returned to sobbing.

Faith waited until she quieted to ask her next question. "If you left a ticket for Oscar and you used the other one, how did your business partner get in?"

Louellyn regarded her as if she thought the question odd. "He had his own ticket. He's staying here."

"Your business partner is attending the retreat?"

Louellyn nodded. "That's actually how he became Oscar's business partner. They're friends because of this whole silly obsession with detective novels. I find the movies mildly entertaining, but I'm not much of a reader."

"Did you tell this to the police?" Faith asked.

The other woman's face creased in confusion. "Tell them what? That I'm not a reader?"

"That your business partner is staying here for the retreat. If your restaurant was having financial problems, your partner would also be someone they'd want to interview."

"Preston would never hurt Oscar," Louellyn said in surprise. "He'd never hurt anyone."

"I'm sure you're right," Faith said. "But the police still might want to know about him. What is Preston's last name?"

"Barnwell. Preston Barnwell." Even as she spoke, Louellyn shook her head slowly. "But suspecting Preston makes no sense. He's one of the most harmless people you'd ever meet. And he was a silent partner, so he didn't get involved in the business that much."

Except financially, Faith thought, *the very area where it's struggling. And he vanished when Oscar's body was discovered.* "Still, the police should know. The more people they investigate, the less they'll be interested in you."

"Do you think so? But it doesn't seem fair to send the police after Preston." Louellyn shuddered. "It's all so overwhelming. Isn't it enough that I have to grieve for my husband without the police treating me like a murderess?"

"I know it's horrible. But I'm sure you want the police to find out who really killed Oscar."

"In that case," a deep, drawling voice said from the direction of the library doors, "it sounds like what you need is a detective."

With a sinking heart, Faith turned in the direction of the voice. A group of manor guests—all wearing trench coats and fedoras—stood just inside the library in a tight cluster. One of the men at the back of the bunch even held a dachshund in a matching fedora.

Faith spotted a few people she recognized from the audience of her speech. The sweet elderly woman in the pink fedora clutched her little fedora-clad Maltese. And the tall, thin, blonde woman stood beside her shorter companion, though his bald head was covered with a fedora today.

The bald man stepped out of the group and continued speaking in his slow, hoarse drawl. "Look, I'm just a lug, but there are things I can do. I can keep my word, I can tail a guy who's walking backward, and I can open a door into a dark room where there's trouble waiting . . . I can't be bought or pushed. Not even for love."

Faith winced, recognizing the speech from her noir research. It was nearly an exact quote from a Philip Marlowe speech in *Poodle Springs*, but the small group clustered around the man nodded solemnly in unison as if it were totally original.

"Same with us," the tall, slender woman piped up from behind him.

Faith gaped at them with no idea of what to say. But she knew one thing for sure. This was all going to go very, very badly.

5

As Faith and Louellyn sat staring at the group of would-be gum-shoes, Watson padded across the room to sit next to the leader.

It's almost like he wants to join them, Faith thought. *Which is the only thing that could make this moment even more ridiculous.*

Steeling herself, Faith stood and walked toward the eager bunch. "We appreciate your concern, but this is a police matter. It's best we leave it to them. I'm certain there are many events planned for this retreat that you will find engaging."

The short, bald man gave her a pitying look. "When a murder is committed, someone needs to pay. And the police only worry about speed. We're here to focus on accuracy."

Again, the rest of the group nodded.

Louellyn walked over and held out her hand. "I don't think I know you."

"Mace," he said. Instead of taking Louellyn's hand, he reached up to touch the brim of his fedora. "Benjamin Mace. 'Occupation: private detective. You know, somebody says, "Follow that guy," so I follow him. Somebody says, "Find that female," so I find her. And what do I get out of it? Ten dollars a day and expenses. And if you think that buys a lot of fancy groceries these days, you're crazy.'"

"You want me to pay you?" Louellyn asked.

"He's quoting Philip Marlowe," Faith explained. She turned to the group. "I know all of you love detective books and movies, but this is police business, and it's serious. I really must ask you to leave it to the police."

The slender blonde woman whose dark eyes seemed too large for her tiny heart-shaped face stepped even closer behind Benjamin Mace.

"Benjamin is an amazing investigator. He's taken real cases before. Not murder, of course, but that doesn't mean he won't be wonderful at that too. The police would be lucky to have his help."

Benjamin gave her a tight smile. "Thank you, Nina. It's nice to hear a kind word now and then."

"I'm sure Mr. Mace is excellent at what he does," Louellyn said. "But I think I'll stick with Faith." She reached out and squeezed Faith's hand. "She *has* solved murders."

The group gawked at Faith in fascination.

"That's not exactly right," Faith stammered. "Please leave this to the police."

A bright beeping sounded from Louellyn's purse. "Oh," she said. "Excuse me just a moment." She stepped away from the group and pulled out her cell phone, speaking into it quietly.

Faith looked over the eager group of would-be PIs with something akin to desperation. If she didn't put a stop to this immediately, Marlene would be furious, and Faith didn't doubt that it would be her fault somehow. "Perhaps you would enjoy browsing the library's collection of mysteries," she suggested to the group. "Our collection includes some rather obscure volumes that would be hard to find anywhere else."

"Thanks for the offer," Benjamin drawled. "But I think we have plans."

"Yes," the silver-haired woman in the pink fedora chirped as she hugged her little dog. "There's a marvelous panel this morning on the perfect femme fatale. I don't want to miss that."

Benjamin glared at the elderly woman. "Mildred, we're on a case."

"Yes, a case," Nina echoed.

"I know," Mildred said. "But I've been looking forward to some of these panels, and so has Sam." She gave her dog a cuddle. "Couldn't we catch some of them?"

"Of course you can," Faith said. She beamed at the older woman. "You don't want to miss that panel. Our luncheon speaker is going to be on it, and I understand she's really wonderful and well-informed on the subject." Actually she didn't know quite that much about it, but she was anxious enough to stretch the truth a little.

"Oh," Mildred breathed. "Cass Morton? I love her books."

"Fine," Benjamin grumbled. "We'll go to the panel, but then we have to get to work."

Faith wished they'd get caught up in the panel discussion and forget about solving the murder, but she didn't have much hope.

She watched bleakly as they turned and marched out of the library. Then she looked around for Watson, intending to pick him up so he couldn't follow the guests, but he was nowhere in sight. He'd pulled another of his impressive disappearing acts.

She turned back to Louellyn as the woman slipped her phone into her purse. Louellyn appeared ashen, and Faith rushed to her side. "Are you all right?"

Louellyn stared blankly at Faith for a moment, then seemed to snap out of a trance. "Yes, I'll be fine. But I have to go. Please find out who killed my husband. And know it wasn't me."

Before Faith could tell her again that she wasn't a detective, Louellyn hurried out of the library, leaving Faith alone with her thoughts and the feeling of impending doom that went with them.

She didn't get much time to dwell on the weirdness of the morning as guests dropped into the library searching for books and gossiping about the events of the night before. Faith assisted them with the books and tried to squelch the gossip without much success. Still, keeping up with the guests made the morning fly by, and soon she was locking up the library for lunch.

She paused to call her aunt to see if Eileen would be coming to the luncheon to hear Cass Morton.

"I wish I could," Eileen said. "But I'm here alone today. Both Gail and Seth called in sick. I've got my fingers crossed for a twenty-four-hour bug because today has been crazy."

Her aunt sounded so stressed that Faith felt bad telling her about Louellyn's husband, but she knew Eileen would want to know.

"How horrible," Eileen said. "I didn't know Oscar as well as Louellyn, but he was always nice to me, and she seemed to be happy with him. The poor dear. I should call her. I'll talk to you later."

Faith ended the call feeling sad. She had an overwhelming urge to get out of the library and decided to sneak down to the kitchen and see Brooke for a few minutes before the luncheon started. Though she knew that the sous-chef would be too busy to sit down with her, she hoped the bustle of the kitchen would actually soothe her nerves.

Then she heard a sound at the terrace doors. As she walked over, she spotted Watson peering through the doors. "So there you are. How did you get outside?" Faith opened the terrace door, and the cat strolled in. That was when Faith realized Watson had something in his mouth.

"What have you caught this time?" she asked, hoping the cat wasn't planning to crunch up a large beetle on the floor. She squatted and removed the object from Watson's grasp. To her surprise, she discovered the thing wasn't an insect of any sort. It was a shiny black gambling chip.

She held it up, studying the detail in the light from the French doors. "Where did you get this, Rumpy?"

Watson's only response was to turn his back on her, as if insulted that she had taken his new toy.

At first, Faith thought the chip must be one the manor had used some time before for a faux riverboat casino night during a previous retreat, but she remembered that those chips were stamped with the image of a wolf. It had been a play on Wolfe's name since he'd dressed up as the riverboat owner. Faith smiled at the memory, even as she wondered at the large bird stamped on the chip. "How odd." Rising, she slipped the chip into her pocket.

Faith considered what to do with Watson while she was gone.

"How about I give you a tunaroon? And another one when I get back if you stay out of trouble."

Watson had looked up sharply at the word *tunaroon*, but she had her doubts about the cat's willingness to stay out of trouble, even as part of a deal.

With a sigh, she headed toward her desk where she'd left the bag of treats.

The cat took his tunaroon as his due, with an air that clearly said his acceptance of it did not guarantee anything on his part.

"Faith, I'm so glad I caught you."

The deep voice coming from above made Faith jump. She glanced up to see Wolfe standing at the railing of the second-floor balcony.

He gave her a sheepish smile. "I'm sorry. I didn't mean to startle you."

"It's not a problem." She managed a cheerful smile. "I'm just not used to anyone coming in the second-floor entrance."

"I've been on the phone all morning, but I wanted to be sure you were all right. I feel like I abandoned you with Mrs. North last night."

"I didn't feel abandoned. You had the whole manor to consider."

"I do appreciate what you did for her. Wait there. I'm coming down." Wolfe backed away from the railing and headed for the spiral staircase. The well-crafted stairs, featuring wrought iron and polished walnut, were almost a work of art.

When he joined her, Faith filled Wolfe in on her conversations with Louellyn as well as the unusual incident with the group of eager guests.

As she spoke, Wolfe's expression darkened. "I'm concerned to hear that. We don't need anyone getting hurt while pretending to be Philip Marlowe."

"I tried to talk them out of it," Faith insisted. "They did head off to one of the panel discussions, but I'm not sure they're going to be easily dissuaded."

"Do you know which guests are involved?"

"I know Benjamin Mace appears to be the leader. I didn't get the full names of anyone else. There was a young woman named Nina who seems to be attached to Benjamin at the hip, an older lady in a pink fedora and a trench coat named Mildred who has a Maltese, and a gentleman with a dachshund in a dark fedora."

"A fedora?" Wolfe repeated. "On the man or the dog?"

"Both."

"I'll see what I can do to cool their enthusiasm. I hope you're not going to take Mrs. North up on her request for *your* sleuthing services. You were a great help in calming a distressed woman, but you certainly know from experience how dangerous it can be to get involved in a murder investigation."

"I promise I don't want to be involved. But I also know from experience that it can be hard to avoid, especially if we're going to have guests running around playing detective."

"I'll make an announcement over lunch to see if we can put a stop to it," he said. "Speaking of lunch, I'm going that way now. Have you eaten? Would you care to join me?"

At the mention of lunch, Faith's stomach growled loudly.

Wolfe laughed. "Shall I take that as a yes?"

Faith felt her cheeks warming, though she laughed along. "I believe so."

"Excellent." He tucked her hand into the crook of his arm and led her toward the library doors.

Faith pointed at Watson as they stepped through. "Stay out of trouble."

The cat yawned.

Somehow Faith wasn't reassured.

Lunches were served in different locations at the manor depending on the kind of retreat. Sometimes the groups were small and intimate, and the banquet hall at Castleton Manor couldn't be described as either of those things.

The manor carefully planned every moment of each retreat to suit the theme and the group taking part. Since the So Noir luncheon was open to anyone in the public with a ticket, they needed a room that could accommodate a large crowd, so they were serving in the banquet hall to show off Castleton at its most impressive. The huge dining room was sumptuously designed and decorated with a soaring ceiling and twelve freestanding gold alabaster columns supporting a swag-covered frieze and cornice.

Seating for the luncheon was at the specially designed immense oak dining table. The chairs were as gorgeous as the table, with padded seats and backs in ruby-colored brocade. The table and chairs always reminded Faith of a medieval tale of castles and knights. A few small tables had been brought in as well, so that the guests who weren't comfortable sitting with a large group could have a more private, if less impressive, place to dine.

When Faith and Wolfe entered the room, most of the attendees were already seated. Faith tugged Wolfe to a stop when she spotted a group of familiar faces. She nodded at Benjamin and a nervous-looking Nina. They were talking to Marlene in low voices.

"That's Benjamin Mace," Faith told Wolfe. "And the woman's name is Nina, but I don't know her last name."

"I think we'd best rescue Marlene before she nips one of them on the nose," Wolfe said.

"In that case, aren't we rescuing them?" Faith retorted.

He grinned and crossed the room in quick strides that left Faith trotting to keep up.

They reached the trio just as Benjamin leaned in toward Marlene and drawled, "'Now I know this is going to sound kind of radical, but did it ever occur to you that it might make things easier if you told the truth occasionally?'"

"I beg your pardon!" Marlene gasped. "I do not lie."

"That's a quote," Faith interjected. "Philip Marlowe said it. Mr. Mace has an amazing memory for quotes."

Marlene's attention snapped toward Faith with a speed that didn't bode well for her temper, but when she saw Wolfe, she froze.

"I'm always happy to meet a fellow fan of Philip Marlowe," Wolfe said. He held out a hand. "How do you do? I'm Wolfe Jaxon."

"Oh, what a wonderful name," Nina gushed from where she stood next to Benjamin, anxiously wringing her hands. "Wouldn't that be a marvelous detective name?"

Benjamin frowned, ignoring Wolfe's hand. "I don't know. It sounds so aggressively masculine."

"I know," Nina breathed, her eyes wide. "Like Sam Spade."

Benjamin folded his arms over his chest and glared at Wolfe. "I'm Mace. Benjamin Mace—"

Nina jumped in before he could launch into the quote he'd given earlier in the library. "I'm Nina Borz. Are you going to be one of the guest speakers?"

"Hardly," Marlene said coldly. "The Jaxon family owns Castleton Manor."

"But we do have an excellent guest speaker for the luncheon," Wolfe said. "I believe you may be familiar with Cass Morton. She writes the Dizzy Dame series."

"Yeah, I've heard of those books." Benjamin rolled his eyes. "A detective dame. Raymond Chandler would turn over in his grave."

"I don't know," Nina said. "Women can be good detectives."

"Sure they can," Benjamin scoffed.

Nina frowned at him. "That's not nice."

"'I don't mind if you don't like my manners,'" Benjamin said, lapsing into another quote. "'I don't like them myself. They are pretty bad. I grieve over them on long winter evenings. I don't mind your ritzing me or drinking your lunch out of a bottle. But don't waste your time trying to cross-examine me.'"

"You certainly have an impressive memory," Faith said.

"He does," Nina agreed with enthusiasm, but then she pouted. "But he's not right about women detectives."

"I believe Ms. Morton is going to speak on the topic of female investigators today. Shall we take a seat?" Wolfe herded Benjamin and Nina toward the table. "Lunch will be served soon."

Once he'd gotten the two guests seated, Wolfe led Faith to two empty chairs some distance down the table. "I need to speak to everyone. I'll join you shortly." Then he stepped up to the podium that faced the end of the table where no one was seated. He spoke quietly to a woman who stood shuffling through a stack of notes.

Faith assumed the woman was Cass Morton. The author had short black hair and cat-eye glasses rimmed with the same black shade. She stood about shoulder height to Wolfe and lifted her chin in a forceful way as she listened to the man who ran Castleton Manor.

Faith felt a wave of gratitude toward the author for showing up for her speech. She definitely didn't want any more surprise speaking jobs during this retreat.

Finally, the woman stepped away from the podium with her notes in her hand.

Wolfe tapped the microphone to get the audience's attention. Then he greeted everyone warmly. "I'm sorry to say that we've already seen tragedy here," he said solemnly. "Last night a local business owner's body was found on the property. The police are investigating. Now, I know many of you are well versed in investigative methods, but I ask you to please focus your energy and attention on the retreat. Leave the police business to the police. I assure you that the Lighthouse Bay Police Department is more than up to the job."

The murmur from the table didn't sound promising to Faith, but at least no one spoke up in open defiance.

After thanking everyone, Wolfe turned the mic over to the author and joined Faith at the table.

Faith split her attention between a savory lunch—featuring perfectly seasoned grilled chicken on a bed of greens—and the fascinating speech about the evolution of the hard-boiled detective from an aggressively male occupation to one more open to creative interpretation. Though

Faith had learned much of the information during her own research on the genre, she enjoyed hearing Cass Morton's thoughts about the creation of her tough female PI.

Faith considered all the times she'd found herself in the middle of investigations since taking the job at Castleton Manor. In some ways, she had a few things in common with the character Cass described. She also often operated on instinct, though she was far from the lone wolf Cass talked about. Faith would be lost without the dear friends she'd made in Lighthouse Bay.

As she thought about her friends, she suddenly had a question for Wolfe. She waited until Cass finished her speech and accepted her applause with a tight smile. Then, when Marlene stepped up to the microphone to make a few quick announcements about the schedule, Faith leaned over to Wolfe and said, "Oscar North's business partner was sitting with Louellyn when I gave my speech last night. But once the body was found, he seemed to disappear. Do you know what happened to him? His name is Preston Barnwell."

Wolfe chuckled softly. "It didn't take you long to discard my warning about not getting involved in a murder case."

"It's not that," she protested. "I just wondered about it because Louellyn told me he's a guest at the manor. Considering his business partner was murdered, maybe someone should make sure he's all right."

"That doesn't sound unreasonable," he said. "I'll have Marlene find his room and send someone to check on him."

"Good. It seems strange to me that he didn't come in to see Louellyn last night after Oscar's body was found."

"I'll look into it. But please don't get involved in this. I can't very well expect our guests to stay out of it if you don't."

"No involvement. Just curiosity." Faith's mind wandered back to her meeting with Louellyn. Somehow she felt at least partially responsible for the woman since Louellyn was an old friend of Eileen. Plus, she couldn't be sure that Louellyn and Oscar would have even been at the manor if Faith and Eileen hadn't gone to Driftwood and reminded them about So Noir. She felt as if she owed Louellyn something. Not a full-blown investigation, of course—the local police were more than competent—but at least some comfort.

Faith made a small inner vow. She wouldn't get involved exactly, but she'd help. A little. Surely that would be fine.

6

After she finished with her announcements, Marlene took her seat on the other side of Wolfe and captured his attention with a long list of things related to the manor. Faith didn't really mind since she wanted to avoid further conversations about staying out of murder investigations.

Faith studied the guests seated at the table. Cass Morton sat across from her but several seats closer to the podium. The author was surrounded by retreat attendees, some of whom held copies of her book. Faith wondered why Marlene hadn't planned an official book signing since that was a normal procedure when they had an author for a guest.

Her musings were interrupted when she heard Wolfe say, "Preston Barnwell." She refocused on their conversation.

"The name doesn't sound familiar," Marlene said, "but this is a large retreat. I'll consult the guest list and get back to you."

"Thank you," Wolfe said. "Once we're certain the man is all right, we'll need to pass the name and room assignment along to Chief Garris."

Marlene wrinkled her nose. "I suppose we must. The quicker the police handle this unfortunate situation, the better." She sighed. "I don't suppose the police would consider not wearing their uniforms when they come to talk to him."

"A man has been murdered," Wolfe reminded her. "The manor will help in whatever way we can, and we will not tell the police how they should handle the investigation."

Marlene sniffed, clearly not enjoying the rebuke in Wolfe's voice. "Of course," she said. "But this is also creating problems for Castleton. Half these people think they're professional investigators. It's going to require extra staff just to keep them out of the cellars and other private areas."

"If you feel we need more staff, then certainly hire them," Wolfe said. He pointedly turned his attention to Faith. "Do you need any extra help? With Mr. North's death happening right outside the library, I imagine that's adding to your workload as well."

"Faith can handle it," Marlene chimed in, despite the fact that Wolfe was clearly not speaking to her. "In fact, she should probably hurry along to reopen the library. Guests so often love to browse the collection after lunch."

Despite the snippy tone in Marlene's voice, Faith knew she was correct. The guests did tend to collect in the library after meals. She placed her napkin on the table. "If you'll excuse me, I'll see to that."

"Before you leave," Wolfe said, "I have a question to ask you. Would you like to go riding with me tomorrow? The head groom has been complaining that several of the horses aren't getting enough exercise. I thought I would go riding along the beach below the manor."

Ignoring Marlene's glower, Faith smiled at Wolfe. "That sounds wonderful. I would love to."

"I need to check my calendar before I'll know exactly when I'm available." He sighed. "Sometimes I feel like my calendar rules my life."

"Since that's settled, I'm sure Faith needs to run along," Marlene insisted.

"I do," Faith said. She wished them both a pleasant afternoon and headed across the long room toward the arched doorway. That was when she noticed Preston Barnwell at one of the small tables.

As she studied the man seated alone at the table, she was struck by how different he was from his business partner. Oscar had been a broad-shouldered man with dark hair and an olive complexion. On the other hand, Preston was unusually thin, which made him appear taller than he was. Faith knew that from having seen him standing beside the statuesque Louellyn the night before. He had nearly colorless hair that was thin enough to show his scalp in places, and his complexion was almost ghostly pale.

Faith paused at the table. "Hello. I'm Faith Newberry. I'm the librarian at Castleton Manor. I wanted to offer my condolences on the passing of your friend Oscar North."

Preston appeared a little startled at the unexpected attention, but he managed a solemn smile. "Thank you. Oscar will be deeply missed."

Faith slipped into the chair next to the man. She knew she was being forward and Marlene would definitely disapprove, but she just couldn't walk away from the opportunity to talk to Oscar's business partner. "I know it must be hard. I saw you with Mrs. North, but I didn't know about your relationship to the deceased. Otherwise, we would have made an effort to support you in this difficult time."

"It was primarily a business relationship," Preston said, shifting in his seat slightly. "Though I am sorry, of course. I still don't know if it was an illness or an accident."

Faith decided not to be the person who told Preston that his business partner had been murdered. "The police haven't released that information yet. I believe you must have been the only person from the opening ceremony who didn't end up on the terrace. Thankfully, I was able to get Louellyn away to the library."

"I *am* sorry I wasn't there to comfort poor Louellyn," he said. "I'd run into her earlier, which is why we were sitting together. I didn't know she and Oscar were coming to the opening event. Then I began to feel unwell. I'm afraid I didn't even make it all the way through your talk. I was disappointed because what I heard was fascinating."

"I'm terribly sorry to hear that," Faith said, wondering if a lingering illness from the night before might be part of what made the man seem so colorless. "Do you need to see a doctor? We have one we can call."

"Thank you, but I'm feeling much better today."

"You mentioned that your relationship with Oscar was mainly professional. I'm surprised because I definitely got the impression from Louellyn that you were old friends."

Preston shrugged. "We got along well enough. Oscar was a bit of a bully. He wasn't mean-spirited, but he had such a big personality that he could run over people. And lately he'd been tense, which made him harder to deal with."

"Tense about money?" Faith asked. She darted a glance back toward the long table, hoping Marlene had not noticed her still in the banquet hall when she should have been opening the library.

"Yes, money was an issue." He exhaled deeply. "As a partner, I was also concerned about the finances, but I hated seeing the strain it put on Oscar and Louellyn's marriage. In my opinion, he was entirely unfair to her. She is not the spendthrift that Oscar made her out to be."

"I got the sense that money was a sore subject between them," Faith commented.

Preston sniffed. "Oscar North never deserved a woman like Louellyn."

From his tone, Faith decided her first impression of the man was correct. He definitely had feelings for Louellyn. "Louellyn is certainly a fine person." On impulse, Faith pulled the gambling chip from her pocket and set it down on the table in front of him. "Have you seen this before? It was found outside, and I wondered if it might have been Oscar's."

Preston stared at the chip as if it might snap at him. Finally, he seemed to shake off his surprise. "I have no idea where the chip could be from. Perhaps it was part of a new promotion idea for the restaurant. Oscar was always creative with promotions."

Though the answer sounded reasonable, Faith had the distinct impression that it was a lie.

The cat watched his human with some alarm. His senses told him the other human at the table was bad news. That person might be baring his teeth in the weird way humans did when they wanted to be friends, but

the cat smelled a rat. And if there was one thing he trusted completely, it was his ability to deal with rats.

Unfortunately, his human was doing what she always did—plunking herself right in the middle of danger. It was up to the cat to save the day. He sneezed in derision. What else was new?

He padded over and leaped up onto the table. As always, his landing was perfect, but he intentionally scrabbled at the tablecloth as if he needed to catch his balance. He accidentally on purpose bumped into the water glass near the ratlike human. The glass overturned, drenching the man in icy liquid.

The human leaped to his feet, giving a satisfying shout of annoyance and shock. He knocked over his chair in the process.

The cat's human scooped him up from the table, which put the detective cat in exactly the right spot to reach out and rake his claws over the other human's arm. He'd show the stranger that his human was protected.

The cat's claws caught in the loose fabric of the man's sleeve. Alarmed at feeling his paw caught, the cat jerked upward, dragging the sleeve along with him. This movement revealed a wide bandage on the man's arm.

A clue! It had to be a clue.

Faith pried Watson's claws loose from Preston's sleeve. She felt caught between horror at what Watson had done and curiosity about the thick gauze bandage that was wrapped around Preston's forearm. Could the man have been injured the night before?

He hastily tugged his sleeve back down.

"I'm so sorry, Mr. Barnwell," Faith said. "Watson gets a little rambunctious sometimes. Did he hurt you?"

"No." He picked up his napkin and dabbed at his pants. "It was more surprising than anything. I believe I would like to be left alone now."

"Of course," Faith said. "Again, I'm so sorry."

Preston turned his gaze to the blackbird gambling chip on the table and shuddered. "Please excuse me. I will need to change before the next event." He rushed away.

Holding Watson closely, Faith looked down at the dark spot on the crisp white cloth. That gambling chip had definitely spooked Oscar's business partner. As she returned it to her pocket, Faith wondered why.

7

To Faith's surprise, she managed to get out of the banquet hall without a lecture from Marlene. The rest of her day was spent talking about books with guests and fending off the occasional question about the night before. Faith didn't get any more visits from Louellyn or Benjamin, and she even had a little time to do some final polish on her talk about vintage noir books as collectibles for the next day. She was starting to hope for the beginning of a normal retreat.

But then Officer Mick Tobin peered at her through the library doors.

With a sigh, Faith raised a hand to wave him in. She liked the thickset officer. He had a good sense of humor, but he definitely signaled the end of her hopeful pretense that everything was back to normal.

"You looked so studious that I hated to bother you." The officer ran his fingers through his short blond hair. "I'm doing follow-up interviews with several of the guests here. Pardon me for saying this, but some of these folks are rather odd."

"It's a noir retreat, and you're a police officer," Faith said as she tucked a slip of paper into the book she was reading. "You have to expect a little bit of strangeness."

"I expect at least a little bit of strangeness every time I come here," he remarked, then shoved his hands into his pockets. "What can you tell me about last night?"

"Well, I knew the man who died," Faith said. "I had met him, anyway. I ate lunch at his restaurant yesterday with my aunt, and he came out to talk to us because his wife knows my aunt. He seemed nice enough, friendly."

"Did you see Mr. North at the manor?" Tobin asked.

Faith shook her head. "I saw his wife during my speech, but he never came into the gallery. At least I never saw him."

"So you don't know what he was doing up here?" the officer asked.

"I assume he planned to join his wife but something kept him from doing it. Is it true that you believe it was murder?"

Tobin shrugged. "We haven't made a definitive statement. He died from a fall from the balcony above the terrace."

"It's not that far."

"Yeah, the medical examiner said that wouldn't normally be fatal, though it might result in broken bones. But apparently the victim struck one of the stone benches on his way down."

Faith winced. *How horrible.* "I think those are all the details I need. Maybe more than I need."

"Sorry. I went up to the balcony. That railing is high. I can't see anyone accidentally falling over it unless he had climbed up on it for some reason."

"Why would Mr. North do that?"

Tobin shrugged again. "Suicide?"

"From a balcony only one floor up? It doesn't sound too effective."

"Or else he was lucky," the officer said. "Or unlucky. The chief wonders if maybe the victim might have been trying to avoid someone and was betting he could jump safely from the railing."

The reference to betting and luck reminded Faith of something. She reached into her pocket and pulled out the poker chip. Handing it over to Tobin, she explained how she came to be in possession of it.

"That's one interesting cat you got there." Officer Tobin turned the chip over and over in his hands. "I'm not sure we need clues dug up by pets for this case, but you never know. I'll give it to the chief."

"Do you mind if I take a photo of it first?" Faith inquired. "I've been asking around about it."

Tobin held out his hand, displaying the chip in the center of his palm. "Sure, just let me know if you learn anything significant."

Faith grabbed her phone and took a photo. From the officer's casual tone and the fact that he didn't slide the chip into an evidence bag, she suspected that he wasn't going to take it seriously. She doubted he would have taken it at all if she didn't have a history of helping the department. Or at least stumbling into things in a helpful manner.

Tobin pointed at the copy of *The Maltese Falcon* on Faith's desk. "Do you know how Sam Spade died?"

Faith raised her eyebrows. "No." She didn't realize the author had killed off the character. She felt a flutter of alarm. Was there some research she'd overlooked?

"He was on a cruise and the ship sank," Tobin said. "But we know his last words." His mouth quirked upward despite his obvious effort to keep a straight face.

Faith folded her arms over her chest. "Really? And what were his last words?"

"'Here's lookin' at you, squid.'" Officer Tobin burst into laughter.

Though it was a terrible pun, Faith couldn't help but smile at Tobin's enjoyment of his own joke.

While she'd been talking quietly with the officer, a few guests had drifted in, but since they'd shown no sign of needing her, she'd let them browse without intervention. When Tobin told his joke, she distinctly heard giggling from behind a shelf of books.

"Well, I'd better get back to the salt mines," Officer Tobin said. "I'll let you know if the blackbird turns out to be a clue."

As soon as the police officer left the library, a guest who'd been examining one of the older copies of *The Big Sleep* put the book down and approached Faith. The man was good-looking with artfully styled dark hair and pale blue eyes. He held out a hand. "Miss Newberry, I wanted to introduce myself. I'm Jordan Pointe. I own Spooks, Spies, and Private Eyes in Boston."

Faith shook the man's hand and smiled. "I'm not familiar with that shop, though I love the name. Is it a bookstore?"

"It is," Jordan said. "We're new, but you watch. We're going to be the next big thing. Genre is where the sales are these days, and everyone loves a good mystery or a gripping thriller." He waved a hand around the room. "I must say, this must be the most extraordinary library I've ever seen."

"It's a marvelous place to work," Faith agreed. "Are you enjoying the retreat, Mr. Pointe?" She nearly flinched as soon as she'd asked the question that was almost automatic. A death occurring during a retreat made her sensitive of everything she said.

"I am," the man said. "And please call me Jordan. We bibliophiles must stick together. This is my first noir event, and I must say, you've gone above and beyond to give us a real murder mystery." He winked.

Faith frowned at the man's casual suggestion that a man's death might be a form of entertainment. Her impression of Mr. Pointe certainly took a dive with that remark. "We're all upset at having a death here." Her tone was colder than she'd intended.

"But not overly surprised, I assume."

Faith stared at him in shock.

"You have to admit, this isn't Castleton Manor's first dead body," he persisted.

"A great many people pass through Castleton Manor," Faith said stiffly. "As with any popular public venue, we've had our share of tragedy. But it isn't something one becomes used to or amused by."

"Now I've offended you," Jordan said. "I am sorry. I'm always putting my foot in it." He smiled. "I promise I will stay far away from the murder investigation. I'm here for the panels and talks. For instance, I enjoyed your talk last night very much."

"Thank you," Faith said. Before she could say more about the speech, Benjamin burst through the library doors and glanced around. Faith nearly groaned as the man spotted her and rushed over.

"I heard you found a clue," Benjamin announced.

"Excuse me?"

"The blackbird," he said urgently. "I heard you found the blackbird. That has to be a clue."

"It was just a poker chip," Faith said. "And I don't even know where it came from. My cat found it."

"Still, I need to see it," Benjamin insisted. "It's the best clue anyone has found so far."

"Mr. Mace," Faith said plaintively, "the retreat is going to have a wonderful mystery dinner and some locked-room activities. Can't you occupy yourself with those and leave this crime to the police? It's not like they've asked for anyone's help."

"They haven't asked, but I'm sure you remember that Louellyn North has." Benjamin drew himself up. "'You know, some cases of murder start when that door there behind you opens up and a fellow rushes in all covered with sweat and confusion and fills you full of bad dope about the setup. But some cases, like this one, kind of creep up on you on their hands and knees and the first thing you know, you're in it up to your neck.'"

Again Faith recognized the Philip Marlowe quote. It was from the film *Lady in the Lake*. Benjamin Mace undoubtedly spent a lot of time memorizing lines from movies and books.

"Actually," Jordan interjected, "this case did rush in all covered with sweat and confusion, right in the middle of Miss Newberry's speech." He eyed the balding man and gave a wry smile. "'So you're a private detective. I didn't know they existed, except in books, or else they were greasy little men snooping around hotel corridors. My, you're a mess, aren't you?'"

Faith couldn't believe that Jordan had responded by quoting from *The Big Sleep*. She knew that Benjamin wouldn't allow the other man to have the last word.

Sure enough, Benjamin gave the tall, handsome bookseller a fierce scowl, added a Bogart growl, and said, "'I'm not very tall either. Next time I'll come on stilts, wear a white tie, and carry a tennis racket.'"

Jordan laughed. "Touché! You do know your film quotes."

At that Benjamin simply turned his back on Jordan. "The police have cleared the second-floor balcony for use again," he informed Faith. "I intend to examine it. Would you like to come along?"

"No," Faith said firmly. "I've been on the balcony many times. I see no reason to examine it again."

"I see every reason," Benjamin said. "If the police closed the balcony, they must believe the murder took place there."

"If there was a murder."

"You disappoint me, Miss Newberry, and that's hard to do with what I've seen and what I've done. But you've done it."

"Now that's not a quote I'm familiar with," Faith said. "Who said that?"

The bald man smiled. "Why, Benjamin Mace, of course." Then he spun on his heel and stalked out of the library.

Faith sighed. It seemed to be her day to be the punch line in other people's jokes. She turned to say something to Jordan, only to find the bookseller had left as well.

She looked around. It was nearly time for dinner, and the room was empty. Faith went over to straighten the display of noir books, thinking that she'd set the library in order and close up for the night. She'd try to get to bed early so she'd be well rested for her presentation in the morning and horseback riding with Wolfe in the afternoon.

Faith shook her head as she imagined what Brooke and her other friends would say about Wolfe inviting her to go horseback riding. They already teased her about Wolfe, claiming that he was around more often since Faith had started working at the manor. Faith didn't believe it was true. And as for tomorrow, she was just helping a friend exercise the horses.

As she collected stray books by the armload, she kept an eye out for Watson. The cat sometimes napped on empty spots on the shelves, and she knew better than to think there would be any point in calling him. Simply knowing she wanted him seemed to trigger the cat's independent streak.

Then Faith remembered that she had a secret weapon. She hadn't given Watson his second tunaroon. The smell of the treat was sure to bring him out of hiding. As she walked toward her desk, she was surprised to hear the library door open. It was rare for a guest to miss the beginning of the dinner hour to browse books.

She turned to see Cass Morton, the author from the luncheon. Faith smiled at her. "I'm surprised you're still here. I thought you were only coming in for the speech."

Cass shook her head. "I decided to stay over and get some writing done. Thankfully, the manor was able to accommodate me. At first Ms. Russell didn't think that would be possible since I'm not interested in the noir events, but Mr. Jaxon rescued me."

"He's good at that," Faith said with a grin.

Gazing around the library, Cass gave a low whistle. "What an amazing collection. I'm trying to imagine what my main character would think of this place."

Faith smiled. "I imagine she'd say, 'The woodwork glowed with the hands of a hundred women, all careful to stay out of the bright lights while they made the world decorative for mankind.'"

Cass laughed and clapped softly. "You've read the Dizzy Dame series."

"All of them," Faith admitted. "I find them a refreshing antidote to the usual noir pessimism and gloom. And my aunt is a huge fan as well. She's the head librarian at the Candle House Library in downtown Lighthouse Bay."

"I'll have to drive in and meet her. I do enjoy chatting with fans." She sighed. "But I'm not sure all the attendees at this particular event consider the series to be properly noir. Female private eyes seem to offend the hard-core fans."

"Well, I definitely love Maddy Dame," Faith said. "Even with her slight cynicism, I think she has some fantastic things to show us about the world while she turns a genre on its ear."

"You've made my day," Cass said. "Could I possibly talk you into having dinner with me?"

Faith was certainly tempted, but she knew she'd be better served by a quiet evening. "I would love to, but I have a presentation tomorrow so I really should get home."

"I understand," Cass said agreeably. "I've done enough book talks to know how much it helps to be well rested. I'm staying for several days, so perhaps we can share a meal at some point while I'm here."

"That sounds nice," Faith agreed. "Now I must call a cat."

Cass laughed again. "Surely you know how well that works."

"I have special abilities." Faith pulled the bag from the drawer of her desk and opened it up to release the smell of tuna. She shook it gently. "Watson!"

Both she and the author glanced around expectantly. Faith listened for the sound of Watson jumping down from whatever shelf he was using for a nap. But the huge library was silent.

"You really had me convinced you were going to do a magic trick," Cass said.

"I'm afraid my cat has snuck out of the library. I'll have to track him down after I close up."

"That sounds like my cue to leave," the author said. "Though I would appreciate it if you'd let me grab a book first. When I'm done writing for the day, I like to read."

"Of course. Please take your time."

Cass browsed the display of mystery novels and picked one quickly, then bid Faith a good night before slipping out of the library.

Faith finished closing up and wondered which way to go to look for Watson. She wasn't in the mood for a full-on search, but she also didn't want to leave him behind to wreak havoc on the manor.

She glanced hopefully through the terrace doors. He could be outside soaking up the last rays of sun for the day. It was one of his favorite pastimes. "You'd better be out there," she muttered. "Or no tunaroon for you since you didn't hold up your end of the bargain."

She stepped out into the warm evening and peered around. She didn't see Watson on any of the marble benches or sitting sphinxlike on the railing, two of his favorite spots.

With a stir of unease, she walked over to the shadow of the upper balcony. *Where is Watson? And why do I suddenly feel so worried?*

8

From the shadows just beyond the door, the cat contemplated the dark corners and cracks of the balcony. Truth always hides in the shadows, he thought, and the hapless humans bumble around, hoping to trip over it. *The short human sweating in the long flapping coat was a case in point. So far, he hadn't even knelt down from the gawky height from which humans viewed the world.*

The cat wondered how humans ever managed to discover anything, since they so rarely got down to ground level where all the best clues hid. As fond as he was of his own person, the cat knew she was just as bad. She was an excellent feeder and cuddler, but she would be hopeless without him to guide and protect her.

As he pondered the sad plight of humans, the cat stared fixedly at an interesting shiny thing caught in the chipped bottom corner of the balcony rail support. He would nab it when the slow-moving human on the balcony turned his back, then deliver it to his human. He wasn't interested in boosting some other would-be detective's ego.

As soon as the cat saw his chance, he darted out of the shadows and seized the shiny thing with his teeth. It was stuck tight in the crack, but cats are not quitters, and soon he pried it loose. With a smug twitch of his stumpy tail, the cat held his head high and trotted toward the balcony door.

"Hey there!" the short human shouted. "What do you have?"

Rats, *the cat thought.* Busted. *There was nothing to do but make a run for it. Luckily, he was not only smart and handsome but fast too. Though the human reached out to grab him, the cat slipped through his meaty fingers with ease.*

The cat was so amused by the foolish human's attempts to catch him that he intentionally slowed down, letting the wannabe detective chase

him around a little. It was fun. He kept it up until the short man was
wheezing and whistling like a teakettle. It was time to finish this game
and get downstairs to his human.

The cat raced down the hall, but another human blocked his way.
The cat didn't like the smell of this one. This person smelled like death and
trouble. A cat knew when something was just plain wrong, so he turned
around sharply, skidding on the smoothly polished floor, and dashed back
toward the balcony.

The short human whooped, obviously thinking he'd finally catch the
detective cat.

Silly human! *The cat darted between the man's legs and out onto*
the balcony. From there, he squeezed between two of the balcony rails
and jumped.

Faith stood on the terrace with her hands on her hips, torn
between worry and frustration. Why did that cat always disappear
when she wanted him most? "Come on, Watson," she grumbled. "I
want to get home."

The words were barely out of her mouth when something hit
her shoulder, something with claws. Faith shrieked as Watson dug
in his claws for an instant before leaping from her shoulder to the
bench beside her.

Gasping from the shock, Faith looked down at Watson's innocent
face. "You nearly gave me a heart attack. Lucky for you I still have my
jacket on. If you'd drawn blood, there would be no tunaroons for you
anytime soon."

"Is that your cat?"

Faith shielded her eyes against the sun and glanced up into the
sweaty face of Benjamin as he peered over the balcony rail above her.

The man needs to get out of the heat in that coat, Faith thought. She knew the evening might eventually cool down enough for sleeves, but they were still months away from trench coat weather.

"If that is your cat, he's stolen a clue," Benjamin said.

"And if he isn't my cat?" Faith asked. "Would it still be theft?"

Benjamin appeared bewildered for a moment, then pointed at Watson. "He took a clue. You need to see what it is."

Faith knelt next to the bench. Sure enough, Watson dropped a shiny bit of metal on the bench beside him and batted at it with his paw. She grabbed it before he could knock it to the ground, then held it up to the light.

"What is it?" Benjamin called down.

"A college fraternity pin," she replied. "I don't suppose you lost yours."

He wrinkled his nose. "I wasn't really the fraternity type in college. I expect it's something the killer lost when he was wrestling with the victim."

"You seem to have developed quite a theory with no actual facts," Faith said. "I doubt the pin has anything to do with the murder or the police would have found it. They already searched the balcony. As you pointed out, they had it closed off for a while."

Benjamin shrugged. "I already searched it too and discovered nothing. Apparently, it took a cat to find it. But it's still a clue."

Faith looked down at Watson who gazed at her with an expression that could only be described as smug. Then she turned back to the man on the balcony. "I'll give the pin to the police in the morning. They can decide if it's a clue."

Benjamin didn't seem thrilled with the idea. "Fine. But 'experience has taught me never to trust a policeman. Just when you think one's all right, he turns legit.'" In case she didn't get the reference, he added, "*The Asphalt Jungle.*" Then he tramped inside.

Faith was relieved to see him go because she was getting concerned about how red his face was. She hoped the air-conditioning would cool him down.

She opened her purse to put the pin in but hesitated with her hand inside, her fingers still grasping the pin. If she dropped the tiny pin into the purse, how long was she going to have to spend rooting around for it tomorrow? Faith could just picture Officer Tobin's patient face as he waited for her to dig out another "pet-found clue." With a rueful smile, she deposited the pin into the pocket of her light blazer instead. She'd find a better way to carry the pin to the police station when she returned to the cottage.

Watson trotted along beside her as she headed home. Faith contemplated what she might make for supper. After a long day, she wasn't sure if she wanted some kind of ridiculously indulgent comfort food or if she'd just go with a salad because it was easy and quick.

It wasn't long before the lovely gardens pulled her thoughts away from food. Passing through the Castleton Manor gardens without being entranced by the variety and beauty of the flowers around every bend of the path was simply impossible. As the sun hung low in the sky, shadows pooled under trees and bushes, making pockets of coolness in the summer heat. Faith knew that several guests would make their way out here after dinner to sit on benches and admire the gardens, maybe with a book, before retiring for bed.

As she rounded a corner near a bubbling fountain, she met a guest who appeared anything but content.

Nina Borz caught sight of Faith and hurried over, dragging a scruffy terrier away from sniffing the base of the fountain. The small dog gave his mistress an annoyed look. The woman didn't stop until she was well within Faith's personal space.

Since Watson was not a fan of most dogs, he ran over and hopped up onto the rim of the fountain, out of the little dog's reach. The terrier yapped at the cat in frustration, but Nina didn't seem to notice even when the leash pulled at her arm. Instead, she leaned even closer to Faith.

These noir fans certainly are close talkers, Faith mused as she resisted the urge to back away. She merely smiled. "Good evening, Miss Borz."

"I wanted to let you know that Benjamin and I are on the case," the nervous-looking woman whispered.

"I did get that impression," Faith said quietly. "I just spoke to him. He was hunting for clues on the balcony above the terrace." She didn't add that her cat had discovered the only clue, but she did say, "Please remember that Mr. Jaxon has asked that the investigation be left to the police." She reassured herself that it wasn't hypocrisy if Watson brought her clues.

Nina widened her already slightly bulging eyes. "He was supposed to wait for me. He knew I had to walk Chandler." It was as if she hadn't even heard Faith's reminder.

Faith felt mildly alarmed at the woman's clear distress. "I'm sure he's still searching for clues somewhere. Though if you haven't had dinner yet, you should return to the manor now so you don't miss the seating."

Nina waved that comment away. "Benjamin and I ate already. He says the brain works better when it's well fueled. Well, I must go find him. He needs me." With that, she hauled Chandler away from Watson and scurried back toward the manor.

Faith scooped up the cat. "The fans of noir novels have definitely been interesting," she said as she rubbed Watson's head. "And don't think I didn't see you teasing that dog."

Watson purred in response. He let her carry him most of the way to the cottage, jumping out of her arms only after they'd left the last of the gardens behind.

"Don't run off," she called after him. "I won't go hunting for you, and you'll miss out on begging for bites of my supper."

Watson seemed to ignore the threat entirely, instead galloping along toward the house.

Lodging in the old gardener's cottage was one of the perks of being the librarian at Castleton. Though not far from the mansion as the crow flies, the cottage felt secluded and private, with topiaries and the Victorian garden separating it from the manor. On warm nights,

Faith usually left her bedroom windows open so the soothing sound of the waves hitting the shore could lull her to sleep.

They were halfway across the lawn when Watson stopped suddenly, staring at the entryway to the cottage. Like the rest of the house, the covered entryway to the front door was stone. It offered a welcome protection from inclement weather, but it also made the front doorstep heavily shaded in the early evening.

"What's the matter?" Faith asked as she caught up with the cat.

Watson's fur stood on end, and his tense muscles made him walk stiffly. Faith could hear a low growl rumbling from the small cat's chest.

Despite the warm evening, Faith felt an icy chill creep up her back. What had upset Watson? She studied the shrubs near the front entryway. They were still clearly lit, and Faith could see no sign of anyone trying to use them for cover. She peered toward the corner of the house and wondered if someone could be hiding there just out of sight.

Then she thought of all the times Watson had stared into space when no one was there or yowled over nothing. She was letting herself get all worked up over some cat fantasy. She gave herself a shake. It was still light out, and despite the secluded appearance of her cottage, she knew they were well within screaming distance of strollers in the gardens. She refused to act like some storybook heroine in need of a good rescuing.

Faith marched toward the front door, reaching into her purse for her keys as she went. About the time she'd halved the distance to the front door, what had seemed to be simple dark shadows cast from the stone roof and walls of the entryway became something much more ominous.

A man dressed entirely in black with a ski mask to match leaped out of the entryway.

Shock froze Faith for less than a second, but it was long enough for the man to be nearly on her. She spun to run, sucking in air to shout for help. She'd taken barely a step before the man rushed by her and swiped her purse right out of her hands.

Faith nearly stumbled in shock. Somehow a purse snatcher and Castleton Manor were such an incongruous combination that she actually felt stunned and dizzy by the idea.

On the other hand, Watson was neither shocked nor frozen. He bolted after the thief, springing at the last moment and hitting the man at midthigh.

The man yelped and slapped at the cat even as he tripped over his own feet and fell.

"Watson!" Faith screamed as the cat seemed to vanish under the man's bulk.

The man scrambled up and kept running with the purse in hand, though he was limping slightly.

Faith gave him no more of her attention. The loss of her purse didn't seem important at all when she stared at the ground where the man had fallen.

Watson lay on the grass, dead still.

9

Faith sprinted across the lawn and dropped to her knees beside Watson. She was almost afraid to touch him. What if she hurt him more? She bent over the cat and gently touched his small head. That was when she saw the slight rise and fall of his chest, and she actually whimpered with relief. Whatever was wrong, she was grateful he was alive.

With shaking hands, she retrieved her phone from her jacket pocket and called Midge. Thankfully, the vet answered on the first ring. Faith's hands shook so hard she was afraid she'd drop the phone. "I'm at the cottage. It's Watson," she said, her voice barely a hoarse whisper. "He's hurt. He isn't moving."

"Is he breathing?" Midge asked.

"Yes."

"Is there any blood? Check his mouth."

Faith checked, but there was no sign of blood.

When Midge asked about poison, Faith told her that wasn't the problem. "Someone stole my purse. Watson tried to stop the thief, and the man fell on him."

"I'm just coming out of the Charles Dickens Suite now after tending to a guest's dog. I'll be over in a few minutes. Call the police," Midge told her, then ended the call.

Faith stared at the phone numbly for a moment. *How can the police help Watson?* Then her shocked brain managed to cut through the fog. The stolen purse. She needed to report it. She made the call, tenderly stroking Watson as she did so. As soon as the call was over, she set the phone on the ground beside Watson and prayed.

She was still waiting alone when Watson opened his eyes and meowed plaintively.

"I know," Faith whispered, blinking back the tears in her eyes. She told herself that it was a good sign that Watson was awake. "Midge is coming. It'll be all right."

Watson rolled over to stand.

But Faith lightly rested her hand on his head. "You need to be still."

The cat gave her an irritated look, but Faith continued petting him, and he seemed willing to wait.

He was beginning to show signs of restlessness again when Midge came running out of the Victorian garden with a bag in one hand and another tote over her shoulder. She dropped to her knees beside Faith, panting. "I see he's awake," Midge said. "That's a great sign."

Faith brightened. "I thought so. He wants to get up, but I didn't think he should."

Midge set her bags beside her, and a small dog popped out of one of them.

Faith was a little surprised Midge hadn't left her Chihuahua at the manor, but she suspected Midge never even thought of it in her hurry to get to Watson. Atticus went everywhere with Midge, often dressed in elaborate costumes to match special occasions and Midge's moods. Tonight he sported only a cheerful polka-dot bow tie and his Doggles, the tiny glasses he wore to correct his failing vision.

Atticus bounded over to sniff Watson and received a glare for his enthusiasm.

Watson reached out a paw and pushed on the Chihuahua's nose, though he did it without claws.

Midge ran careful hands over Watson, probing gently for broken bones or signs of internal bleeding.

Watson clearly liked the attention and began purring.

"He's purring," Faith said. "That must mean he's all right."

"It might," Midge said hesitantly, "though a cat in pain will sometimes purr to comfort himself."

Faith wrung her hands as worry swept over her again. *Is Watson in pain?*

"Well, Watson hasn't objected to any of my probing, so I'm inclined to doubt he has anything broken. Trust me, cats let you know if you're hurting them. It's possible he just had the wind knocked out of him. Still, we can take him down to the clinic if you want and get an X-ray." Midge took her hands off Watson.

The cat stood up and shook, as if to shake off all the probing. Then he licked Atticus right on the end of his nose.

The dog jumped back, obviously startled.

"That's a surprise," Faith said. "Could Watson have some kind of brain injury?"

Midge laughed. "I don't think so. His eyes are tracking fine, and he isn't having any balance problems. Maybe he's just finally decided to be pals with Atticus."

Faith doubted that. She suspected Watson was more than a little jealous of the pampered pup, but he certainly wasn't being his usual cranky self toward him. She watched Watson rub his jaw against Atticus's Doggles. "He seems all right."

"Let's see if he's willing to eat." Midge rummaged through her second bag and pulled out a bag of treats.

Both Watson and Atticus snapped to attention as soon as she opened the bag.

Midge held out a treat to Watson, but Atticus leaped in front of the cat and snatched the morsel out of Midge's fingers.

"Atticus! Where are your manners?" Midge scolded.

Watson smacked the little dog on the rump with a paw that included claws this time.

Atticus yelped and backed away.

"You deserved that, young man," Midge said as she handed a treat to Watson.

The cat didn't bother with his usually finicky act and instead gobbled up the treat.

"He's definitely not off his food either," Midge said. "I think he's fine, but keep an eye on him. Call me if he acts oddly at all. We'll meet at my office and get an X-ray."

"I will." Faith scooped up the cat and rubbed his ears.

Watson purred loudly.

Midge reached out and chucked the cat under the chin. "He may be a little stiff and sore tomorrow. He should have a quiet day at home."

"That might be tough," Faith said. "I still haven't figured out how he manages to sneak out of the cottage on a regular basis."

Midge smiled as she gathered up her bags and Atticus. "Just do your best."

Tires crunched on the narrow drive that led to the cottage. A Lighthouse Bay police car pulled into view.

Officer Tobin hopped out of the car, clear concern on his face. "Are you all right?"

Faith nodded. "I might have a bruise where the man jerked the purse away from me, but it's nothing serious. He fell on Watson, though."

A faint smile pulled at the corners of the officer's mouth. "I assume Watson was playing hero. Is he okay?"

"He seems to be fine," Midge reassured him.

"Glad to hear it." Tobin pulled a notepad out of his pocket. "Can you describe the thief for me?"

"He was dressed in black. Black pants, a black hoodie, and a black ski mask," Faith said. "He was taller than me, but he rushed by me so fast that I couldn't say how much taller. I thought he was trying to attack me, so I was running away and didn't get a good look at him. Once he got involved with Watson, I didn't pay attention to much beyond my cat's safety."

"I can understand that," the officer said. "But did you notice anything at all? His skin tone, for instance? Eye color? Voice? Are you certain it was a man?"

"He didn't speak, but I'm pretty sure it was a man. He was wearing gloves, so I don't know what his skin was like." Then she thought of something. "He was limping. He fell, and when he got up, he was limping."

"Well, that's something," Tobin said, but his tone wasn't exactly optimistic.

Faith was grateful that Midge stayed with her during her report to Officer Tobin. He was a nice guy, and Faith liked him, but she was feeling increasingly exhausted now that the adrenaline from the encounter was draining away. When the police car finally retreated down the drive, Faith was trembling slightly from exhaustion, and the evening had progressed to the point where the shadows reached from the house like dark fingers.

"You need to get inside," Midge said, giving Faith a pat on the arm. "Do you want me to come in and fix you something? You could probably use some supper."

"No, I'll be fine," Faith said. "I've kept you long enough. Thank you for everything."

"I'm happy to help. Give me a call tomorrow to let me know how Watson is doing."

"I will," Faith promised.

As grateful as she was to Midge, she was glad to finally be alone as she headed into the cottage. She gave Watson some dinner and fresh water and was relieved to see that the cat dived into both cheerfully. Her gratefulness at how well they'd come through the attack brought tears to Faith's eyes, making her even more aware of how tired she was. She warmed up a can of soup and headed to bed as soon as she'd finished eating.

The morning sun slipped around Faith's blinds and woke her before the alarm in the morning. For an instant, she didn't remember any of the events of the evening before and smiled at the intruding sunbeams. Then Watson stirred beside her on the bed and yawned, showing off a pink tongue and sharp teeth, and the purse snatching came back in a rush.

Faith gently picked up the cat. "How are you feeling?" she asked him.

Watson licked the end of her nose.

She smiled. "I'll take that as a statement of wellness."

As Midge had suggested, Faith left Watson at the cottage, though not without considerable sulking on his part. He'd eaten his breakfast with vigor, but Faith noticed he wasn't quite as quick as usual, and she assumed he was feeling the soreness Midge had warned her about. "I'll check on you later," she said through the door.

She received a disgruntled meow in return.

As Faith walked the paths through the gardens, she noted how discombobulated she felt without her purse. She'd considered carrying a different purse, but since all the things she'd need were in the one that had been stolen, she didn't see the point. She was just grateful she hadn't been carrying any credit cards as she'd not intended to leave the manor property. She would have had to cancel them before getting to bed.

She glanced at her watch as she entered the foyer. If she hurried, she'd have time to grab a cup of coffee. She rushed to the coffee and gift shop.

"Oh, I'm so glad you came in," Iris said. "How is Watson?"

"You heard about Watson?"

"I saw Midge as I was leaving, and she said she was running to meet you. I didn't get many details. If I'd been a bit younger, I would have raced out with her, but I didn't want to slow her down. I assumed something bad had happened from the way she was moving."

"I do appreciate the thought. Watson had a little accident, but Midge believes he'll be fine. I think he might be feeling a bit stiff today, and he definitely didn't like being left behind at the cottage."

Iris chuckled. "When has he ever liked that?"

"True enough. Watson does like to be in the middle of things. Speaking of things, I need to grab a cup of coffee and run. I have a presentation this morning on vintage noir books as collectibles."

Iris poured coffee into a cup. "Sounds fascinating."

"I hope the audience thinks so."

By all appearances, they did, though the group listening was markedly smaller than the one that had heard her keynote. That was fine with Faith. She was happiest when speaking to a small group, so she could make eye contact with each listener. It helped her gauge how the speech was going and whether she needed to pick up the pace or drop in something to dazzle them. The audience in the library seemed attentive all the way through.

Faith did notice that Benjamin was not among her audience, but she spotted Nina sitting near the back, clutching her terrier and watching the door as much as she watched Faith.

Faith felt awful for the woman. It seemed like Benjamin had ducked out on her again. *Probably to search for clues somewhere.* That thought reminded Faith of the fraternity pin, and she gasped in the middle of her presentation, making the audience stare at her quizzically. She covered with a smile and continued talking about collectible books.

She gave herself a mental poke. She couldn't believe Officer Tobin had been right there at her cottage and she'd forgotten to give him the pin. Of course, she had been more than a little rattled by the theft and by Watson's near miss.

When she finished speaking, the small audience rose and began milling around.

Faith noticed that three men in the audience limped. One of the men had a cane, and Faith didn't believe she'd seen him at the manor before. The other two limping were Jordan Pointe and Preston Barnwell. But she couldn't imagine why either of them would want her purse.

Her attention was distracted by the entrance of one of the manor staff. The young man carried Faith's purse.

Faith slipped around the podium and said to the woman who'd been approaching, "Please excuse me. I'll be right back." She reached the young man with the purse. "Where did you find it?"

He handed her the bag. "One of the gardeners discovered it this morning. He said it was shoved into a hedge next to a bench where someone had dumped all the contents. He gathered everything up and put it back in the purse and brought it to the lost-and-found office this morning. We checked the ID in the wallet and saw it belonged to you."

"Yes, it was stolen last night." Faith quickly rummaged through the purse. To her surprise, she didn't notice anything missing. Her wallet with her ID and a bit of cash were still inside. The thief didn't want money, so what had he been after?

She thanked the young man and headed back to chat with the woman who stood next to the podium, waiting patiently.

The woman gushed about Faith's talk and described her own collection of vintage books.

Though there were few topics Faith loved more than books, she had trouble concentrating. Her mind wouldn't let go of the oddity of stealing a purse but not taking anything out of it.

When she finished chatting with the woman, she was surprised to see Jordan waiting to talk with her. "I see you're limping," she commented. "I hope you're all right."

The handsome man blushed and smiled sheepishly. "I fell over a stool in my room and landed on a side table." He sighed. "I chose the Jane Austen Suite because I always admired the author. She seemed like such a sensible, intelligent, no-nonsense person. I guess I didn't expect the room decor to be quite so impractical."

Faith nodded. She'd been in the Jane Austen Suite more than once. It was one of their most lavish and feminine suites with lots of delicate furniture and plenty of pink. "I'm sorry to hear it's been uncomfortable for you."

"It was more uncomfortable for the table," Jordan said. "I may be limping, but I'll recover. However, I'm not sure that table will ever be the same. I assume my room bill is going to be outrageous when I pay for that."

"I can talk to the assistant manager for you," Faith offered, although she didn't necessarily welcome this kind of conversation with Marlene. She couldn't imagine that Marlene would be too sympathetic to the man's clumsiness.

Jordan waved away the offer. "Oh no, that's all right. I should have watched where I was going. It's not like the stool ran out and attacked me."

The remark startled Faith. Was he making a reference to Watson's attack? Could he be the purse thief? He didn't seem like the type, but Faith had learned more than once that people weren't always the way they seemed to be.

"Miss Newberry?"

She started and met the man's concerned eyes.

"I know my joke wasn't all that funny," Jordan said, "but I didn't mean to offend."

Faith forced a smile. "You didn't. I was just reminded of something else." To cover her distraction, she nodded toward Preston. "You aren't the only one limping here today. I wonder if our furniture is more dangerous than I'd thought."

Jordan followed her gaze. "I couldn't say. I have to admit that I don't know a soul here. This is my first retreat. I've wanted to attend one of your retreats for years, but I can't normally get away." Then he chuckled. "Maybe I should start a furniture-fighting support group."

"That would be an interesting addition to the retreat," Faith agreed. She found she was torn between liking Jordan and considering him a suspect. He was friendly and charming. But he was also limping, and his joke was far too close to what really happened. Faith decided to track down one of the housekeepers and find out if Jordan's room really had a damaged table.

"I'll go ask him if he wants to join," Jordan said with a twinkle in his eye, and he turned to walk over to Preston.

As soon as the man left, Nina walked over with Chandler in her arms. "Have you seen Benjamin?"

"Not today," Faith answered.

"He was supposed to be here. He has a small collection of vintage books, and he wanted to hear you speak. I'm worried about him."

"Perhaps he's off sleuthing," Faith suggested.

"No. He wouldn't go off without me again. We talked." Nina hugged the dog in her arms. "But I'm a little worried he's mad at me because of Chandler."

"Because of Chandler?" Faith echoed.

"Chandler is very protective of me. It's just him and me really," Nina said. "And he snapped at Benjamin the teeniest little tiny bit. You'd think I'd gone after him with a chain saw for all the fuss he made. I thought he'd be over it by now. Chandler didn't even draw blood."

"Does Chandler have a history of biting?" Faith asked. "As you may know, the manor's policy allows pets in the public areas as long as they are friendly with people and other pets."

"No, Chandler is a sweetheart," Nina assured her.

Then, as if to give lie to this remark, Jordan returned, and the small dog growled ominously at him.

"Whoa," the tall man said. "It's okay, little guy."

The dog's growl grew louder.

"Miss Borz," Faith said, "it's beginning to look like Chandler has issues with people."

"Chandler doesn't have issues. He loves people," Nina insisted as she clutched the dog tightly.

Jordan pointed at the nearby display of mysteries. "I don't think I've read some of those." He strode away, and the dog stopped growling.

"I'm going to have to insist you keep Chandler in your room if he has so much trouble with people," Faith said patiently. "I know some dogs don't care much for men."

"He's fine," Nina said more firmly. "I'm much more concerned about Benjamin. I have to find him."

"Maybe he simply slept in."

"I went by his room." She frowned. "I know what you're thinking, but Benjamin's not just avoiding me. He may be slightly upset about Chandler, but he wouldn't be cruel, not like that terrible man who was murdered."

Faith raised her eyebrows in surprise. "Oscar North? You knew him?"

"No, but I heard he once played a horrible, cruel trick on Benjamin at one of the noir retreats several years ago."

"Really? What was the trick?"

"He talked Benjamin into playing a dead body for a sleuthing game," Nina replied. "Then he made him take off most of his clothes and lie on the floor, covered in red goo. Only there was no game. And poor Benjamin had to creep back to his room through a crowd of people who saw him in his underwear. Plus, he got into trouble for public nudity."

"Oh, that is awful," Faith said. *And it sounds like a motive for murder.*

"Benjamin tried to tell them the truth, of course," Nina went on. "But that awful man denied everything, and everyone believed *him* instead. If you ask me, they're as bad as Oscar North." She glanced around at the other guests and scowled. "All of them."

As she finished her story, Jordan joined them once more.

Chandler began barking and snarling, so Nina hurried away with the terrier.

Faith watched her go, wondering if Nina's attachment to Benjamin could have motivated her to take part in a murder.

"That dog is a bit of a menace," Jordan said.

"I am sorry about that." Faith's apology faded when she saw Jordan's face as he stared after Nina and her dog. He looked furious. Could he be that upset over a little growling?

"It's not your fault," he said, his expression quickly changing into something far more pleasant when he saw her watching him. "I should be heading to the next event. I don't like to be late."

When he walked away, Faith was left with fresh unease over the charming man. But she didn't have any more time to think about it because Preston limped up to her.

The man's face was nearly as angry as Jordan's had been. "I demand you do something about the police harassing Louellyn North."

Faith blinked at him. "What makes you think I control the local police?"

"Don't you?" Preston asked. "From what I've heard, you control a great deal around here."

"I don't know what your source is, but I assure you he or she is mistaken," Faith said calmly. Then she gestured to his leg. "I notice you're limping today. You weren't the other night. Are you all right? I can call a doctor if you need one."

"I'm fine. I'm also aware that you're trying to distract me, but I'm not going to be diverted." Preston pointed at Faith. "You'd better call off the police, or you won't like what happens." Then he spun awkwardly and limped away.

Faith stared after him, too shocked to respond.

10

Once the library was empty of guests, Faith took a moment to call the police. She leaned a hip against her desk as she waited for the call to be passed along to Officer Tobin.

"Good morning, Miss Newberry," he said cheerfully. "Please tell me you're not calling with a fresh catastrophe. I'm beginning to worry about you."

"No, I actually have good news. My purse was found by a gardener this morning. It was shoved into one of the hedges next to a bench where the thief apparently dumped the contents but didn't take anything. Nothing is missing."

"Nothing?" he asked. "So I take it you didn't have any money in there to begin with?"

"I had about thirty dollars. It's still there."

Officer Tobin whistled. "That's a surprise. Maybe someone disturbed the thief as he was going through the contents, and he abandoned it. So, how's Watson?"

"He seems to be fine today, but that reminds me." Faith took a deep breath, steeling herself for the officer's likely reaction. "Watson found something else yesterday on the balcony. I would have given it to you last night, but I forgot in the shock of the purse snatching and Watson's injury."

"You know, I'm getting teased for how many Watson-found clues I collect," Tobin said. "It's a good thing your cat has such a great track record. What did he find this time?"

"A fraternity pin."

"You should probably bring it in, but there's no hurry. If it's been handled by bare hands and carried around in a cat's mouth, it's not going to have any usable prints."

"Do you want to see the purse too? Maybe check it for prints?"

Officer Tobin sighed. "I'm afraid it has the same problem. It's been handled by you and the gardener and who knows who else. And the chief would never sign off on the lab time for something like this when the property was recovered completely intact."

Faith felt a flare of annoyance. "But Watson could have been killed."

"And that would have been terrible. Really. I like Watson a lot. But lab time is expensive, and the chief has to account for every penny the department spends."

Faith didn't say anything, waiting until she was sure she could speak politely.

"None of this means we won't keep the case open or that we don't care," Officer Tobin said gently. "It could be the beginning of more thefts. Maybe some kind of test run. Who knows?"

Still annoyed, Faith considered mentioning the newly developed limps by Preston Barnwell and Jordan Pointe, but she was worried that Officer Tobin would think she was grasping at straws. "Thank you for responding so quickly last night," she said finally.

"I'm just glad you and Watson are all right," the policeman said. "And I'm glad you got your purse back. I wish every case we handled had such a happy ending."

"Thanks. I'll bring the fraternity pin in tonight after my book club meeting at the Candle House Library."

"I'll look forward to it." Tobin didn't sound eager, but then he admitted, "I'll be here. The chief has us all working late since the death of Mr. North. You know the chief. He takes crime in his town personally. We all do."

Faith felt her annoyance wane when she heard what Tobin and the other officers were going through. "Do you have any leads?"

Officer Tobin laughed. "None I'm likely to share, even considering how much I like you. As the chief says, you're not on the police force yet. But we might have a badge for your cat. He's better than a canine unit."

"Well, I might have a lead. I heard today that a few years ago Oscar North played a vicious and public practical joke on one of the retreat guests." She repeated the story Nina had told her. "I could definitely see how Benjamin Mace might hold a grudge. His friend Nina Borz certainly does."

"That's interesting. I'll check it out," Officer Tobin said. "Now if you'll excuse me, I have a to-do list that would make you weep. I'll see you this evening, Miss Newberry." He thanked her for calling and hung up.

Faith started putting away the books she'd used as samples for her presentation. Though the library had several locked cases for the rarest books of the collection, none of the noir novels qualified. The books had some value, but the Jaxons didn't believe in locking away older books unless they were first editions. Having them on the shelves might be a visitor's only chance to read the books.

She'd just shelved the last book when the library door opened and Louellyn walked in. The woman's gaze swept the library, and then she strode over to Faith. Louellyn's eyes were still a little red, but she seemed much calmer than during her previous visit.

Louellyn caught one of Faith's hands and squeezed it. "I had to come and ask you if you'd learned anything about what happened to Oscar."

"I haven't learned much and nothing really helpful. But I do have something to ask you. A fraternity pin was found on the balcony. Does that sound familiar to you?" Faith wished she had the pin to show her, but she'd left it at home.

Louellyn shrugged. "Maybe. It might have belonged to Oscar. He had a collection of fraternity pins from when he worked for a food service company early in his career. They catered to fraternities exclusively, and Oscar collected pins of all the fraternities he'd ever served."

"That's interesting," Faith said. "He must have loved the job."

"I don't think so. I asked about the fraternity pins a few times, but as much as Oscar loved to talk, he didn't like to talk about them. I don't think they were part of a very happy time."

"Then it seems odd that he would keep them."

"I thought so too. Why hang on to something that makes you feel awful? He keeps the collection in a drawer in his office." Louellyn paused and blinked several times. "Kept, I mean. I suppose I should get used to talking about him in the past tense."

"Do you think I could look at the collection sometime?" Faith said. "To see if there seems to be a pin missing?"

Louellyn smiled. "Of course. I would love to have you over to the house. Perhaps you could bring Eileen. We could have tea. I always loved the English habit of afternoon tea."

"Have you been to England?" Faith asked.

The woman smiled and nodded, and then her expression turned sad again. "I used to travel whenever I could. I made sure to go somewhere new every year, but then we opened the restaurant."

"I have one other thing to ask you about Oscar. Someone told me a story about a previous noir retreat." Faith repeated what Nina had told her, this time trying to put as good a face on it as she could. She didn't want to insult Louellyn's memory of her husband, but Faith definitely had changed her own feelings about Oscar when she'd heard the account.

"I'm not familiar with that specific incident," Louellyn said. "But it sounds like Oscar. He considered himself quite a prankster. He pulled stupid stunts on his crew at the restaurant until we had a sous-chef quit over it. That's when Preston and I put our foot down and insisted his practical jokes didn't belong in a business."

"Were the pranks ever cruel?" Faith asked.

"When I first met Oscar, I thought they were funny. He was always looking for fun or mischief. That's what drew me to him in the first place. But over time, his jokes got old. And sometimes they could be cruel." Her face reddened, and she shook her head, clearly in distress. "I don't want to talk about it. My husband is dead. Why would someone grumble about an old practical joke now? That just sounds petty."

"Perhaps," Faith said carefully. "But it could also be a motive."

Louellyn wrapped her arms around herself as if she were suddenly chilled. "I can't discuss this anymore. I thought I could, but I can't. Thank you for doing what you can. Please keep trying."

Faith reached out a hand and laid it on Louellyn's arm. "Before you go, I have one more question. Are the police still treating you like a suspect?"

"Not really. I don't know. They're sly," Louellyn said. "You never know what's going on behind their professionalism. I suppose that's how people are. Everyone has a mask. It's making me wonder if I can trust anyone."

"I believe the police will find out what truly happened," Faith said.

Louellyn didn't answer but merely nodded. Then she murmured a goodbye and left the library.

Faith wondered how far Oscar's antics might have gone. If the cruelty he'd shown Benjamin had been a common event, it was possible there were many more people with reason to hate Oscar. Could a prank have inspired a murder?

Faith spent the rest of the morning focusing on library business. She met several new retreat guests and had a nice time talking about mysteries. When lunchtime rolled around, she headed down to the kitchen to eat with Brooke and ran into Wolfe.

"I was on my way to the library to speak to you," he said. "I heard about your horrible experience last night. Are you all right? Is Watson?"

"I'm fine, and Watson is having a quiet day in the cottage, per Midge's orders. We'll be going to a book club meeting together later, so perhaps he'll forgive me for leaving him alone all day. I even got my purse back." She explained about the gardener finding the purse with its contents intact.

Wolfe frowned slightly. "I don't like the uncertainty of all that. Why would someone steal a purse and not take the money in it?"

"I spoke to Officer Tobin this morning," Faith said. "His theory is that the thief was possibly interrupted right after dumping out the contents on one of the garden benches and fled to avoid notice."

"I suppose that's possible." Wolfe's frown dissolved into something more rueful. "By the way, I'm afraid I need to put off our afternoon horseback riding. I have a conference call I need to take to deal with some family business."

"That's all right," Faith said. "I have the book club meeting tonight, so it might be better if I don't arrive saddle sore." *I'd never hear the end of it.*

"Has it really been that long since you rode?"

"I'm afraid so," she admitted.

"Then I'll be sure you get an easy mount. So let's plan on tomorrow afternoon." He flicked a glance at his watch and groaned. "I have to run. I need to connect with Marlene before my call. Thanks for being so understanding about the ride."

"It's not a problem. Thanks for including me in it."

As soon as he rushed off, Faith went down to the kitchen. The well-organized bustle of the kitchen made her think of Driftwood, and she wondered about what kinds of tricks Oscar might have subjected his employees to. It wouldn't have been that hard for someone in the kitchen to follow Oscar to the manor.

Brooke rushed toward Faith, handed her a salad, and pointed her toward the small table tucked into the back of the kitchen. "I'm sorry, but I can't sit with you today. One of my assistants is out with a summer cold, and it's been crazy as a result. Plus, one of our guests has an allergy he didn't report, and now he insists we clear every strawberry out of the kitchen. That's nixed two dessert plans, and I'm feeling a bit frantic. We'll talk tonight, okay?"

"Absolutely."

The hard work going on around her made Faith feel slightly guilty, and she returned to the library as soon as she finished the salad. She spent the rest of the afternoon focused on her normal library duties, which was a welcome relief from the drama of the last few days.

When she got home, Watson greeted her with a chorus of annoyed yowls. She was surprised that he was still there, but maybe his stiffness from last night prevented him from being able to perform whatever magic tricks he did to get out of the cottage. Faith bought his approval with a few treats.

After a light dinner, Faith put the fraternity pin in her pocket, and they headed to the book club meeting.

A charming three-story stone building, the Candle House Library had once housed a cottage industry in candle manufacturing until a proper candle factory had been built in the 1840s. Many years ago, the Jaxon family descendants had donated the building to the town for use as a privately funded library. Because it was private, Eileen had unusual freedom in setting rules, so pets were allowed at the book club meetings. Midge always brought Atticus, and Watson tagged along with Faith when it suited his mood.

The old building still had some of the original slightly wavy glass in the windows, which sometimes cast interesting patterns of light on the floors when the sun caught them just right. The library had massive wood beams and a huge stone fireplace where tallow had once been processed. Now the fireplace was the focal point of a cozy reading area, and this was where the book club usually met to chat about everything under the sun, including books.

When Faith and Watson settled into one of the comfortable chairs next to Midge and Atticus, she immediately realized that books were not going to be the top discussion point for the night.

"How is Watson feeling?" Midge asked as she leaned over to rub the top of Watson's head.

"He seems to be fine. Just a little cranky from being left in the cottage all day," Faith said. "But he's stuffed full of treats, because I'm not above bribes."

"Sometimes bribes are the best choice," Midge said.

Brooke plucked a strawberry cookie from the tray Eileen had set out. Faith suspected the cookies themselves were Brooke's contribution, considering that she had to get all the strawberries out of Castleton's kitchen. "I know I'm open to bribes, especially if they're chocolate." Brooke shook a finger at Faith. "And don't think I'm not annoyed to learn you didn't call me after you were robbed."

Faith's aunt Eileen sat in the fourth chair. The soft click of her knitting needles paused as she gave Faith a reproachful look. "As an actual blood relative, I might have liked to hear about it firsthand myself."

"I'm sorry. I was exhausted afterward and went straight to bed." To make up for it, Faith ran through the details and added the weirdness of getting her purse back with all the contents intact. "Officer Tobin thinks the thief must have been frightened away right after he dumped out the purse, or I'd probably have lost my wallet."

Brooke's eyes shone with curiosity. "So do you think the purse incident has anything to do with the murder?"

Faith picked up a cookie and nibbled on it. "That seems unlikely."

"I heard that Louellyn came to talk to you," Eileen remarked. "I do appreciate you helping her worry less."

"I'm happy to help her," Faith said. "Though I think she was worrying needlessly. I don't believe the police consider her a serious suspect."

Eileen's knitting needles clicked furiously for a moment, a sign that she was thinking. Then she paused, clearly having made a decision. "I hate the idea of gossiping in the midst of this, but I'm afraid the police interest in her might be more than you think. I've been aware of some tension between Oscar and Louellyn. I always thought it might be about Preston Barnwell. It's obvious that Preston has feelings for Louellyn. It's all over his face every time they're together."

"I wondered about that," Faith said. "Mr. Barnwell was rather . . . aggressive with me today over Louellyn. He seemed to think I might have some control over the Lighthouse Bay police."

Eileen lifted her eyebrows. "Was he threatening?"

"Vaguely," Faith replied. "Do you think he and Louellyn might have been having an affair? Or perhaps they had one in the past? Louellyn didn't seem all that friendly to the man on the night Oscar died."

"I don't know," Eileen said. "I prefer to think not. Louellyn did seem to genuinely love Oscar."

Faith nodded, remembering how devastated Louellyn had been when Oscar died. Faith doubted the woman was a good enough actress to fake that. "I wonder if Oscar might have noticed his business partner's affections toward his wife. I can't imagine he would have liked that."

"I can't see how Oscar could have missed it," her aunt said. "But you never know what spouses might be aware of."

"All the more reason why I don't have a husband," Brooke chimed in. "I find Diva and Bling to be enough drama for me." Brooke's two angelfish lived quite emotional lives, at least according to Brooke.

Everyone laughed.

"How did your cleansing of the kitchen go?" Faith asked. "Are you free of strawberries?"

Brooke grinned. "The kitchen is, but even after baking cookies, I still have cartons of strawberries at home. I need to get them in the freezer before I go to bed tonight."

Eileen paused in her knitting again. "You could make jam. I have a great refrigerator jam recipe."

"Take her up on the offer," Faith insisted. "I've had that jam. It's fantastic."

"Then I'll take it." Brooke groaned and stretched. "But I'm still irritated that we had the problem in the first place. It ties our hands if the guests don't reveal their allergies, and this guy is a businessman. He must travel. Does he do this to kitchens everywhere?"

"Some people do seem to feel entitled," Midge said. "I suppose anyone who works with the public has horror stories."

"No doubt," Brooke agreed. Then she turned a mischievous grin on Faith. "I hope you'll keep me in mind if you do any sleuthing. I do hate to miss an adventure."

"I wish I could miss the one I've already had." Faith looked down at the cat curled up in her lap. "You can't believe how terrified I was when Watson lay so still on the ground. And all because he was trying to protect me."

Brooke's smile slipped away. "That must have been horrible."

Midge leaned over and stroked Watson's head, getting a purr in response. "Our little hero."

Atticus gave a sharp bark, as if in agreement. But Faith suspected it was more likely out of jealousy.

Midge's comment led to the whole group making a fuss over Watson, which he ate up.

After that, the conversation moved on to other local topics before sliding into a few minutes of actual discussion of the books they were all reading. Faith's reading time had been taken up with her preparation for the noir retreat, so she mostly listened to the others and made a mental note of books that sounded interesting.

When the book club finally concluded for the evening, Faith began helping Eileen clean up. Then she yelped. "I almost forgot that I promised Officer Tobin I'd drop off the fraternity pin that Watson found on the balcony."

"What fraternity was it?" Eileen asked.

"Not one I'm familiar with," Faith said. "But I never paid much attention to fraternities in college." She reached into her pocket and held out the tiny pin.

Eileen squinted at it. "I can't tell much about it right now. Let me get a picture of it, and I'll do some research when I get time tomorrow."

"Thanks. That sounds good." Faith waited while Eileen took the photo, and then she left with Watson in her arms. The cat squirmed as she crossed the dark parking lot. "Forget it," she told him. "I don't need to lose you out here."

But Watson was a superior escape artist and soon wriggled free, jumping gracefully to the pavement. As soon as his paws hit the ground, he began to growl, his fur standing on end.

"What's wrong?" Faith asked.

Watson stalked toward the shadows.

A dark figure stepped out into the light cast by the nearest lamppost. "Miss Newberry," the stranger said, his voice deep and rough, "you should restrain your pet. We wouldn't want him to get hurt."

11

With a cry, Faith grabbed Watson, not wanting a repeat of the night before. She raised her chin as she faced the man standing in the pool of light. "What do you want?" she demanded, proud that her voice didn't shake.

"No need to be alarmed," the man said. He was only medium height, but somehow he seemed looming and dangerous as he watched her through narrowed eyes. "I'm simply a businessman. I believe you have something that belongs to me."

"That seems unlikely, since I've never seen you before," Faith said, although she immediately thought of the fraternity pin in her pocket.

The man smiled, but it didn't make him appear any friendlier. He reminded her of a storm cloud waiting to discharge lightning on anything that annoyed it too much. "I'm Michael Burke, and I was told you'd found one of my markers. I give them to very special clients. It's a round token with a blackbird on it." He held up thick fingers spread apart to illustrate the size of the blackbird chip.

"My cat found one of those chips at Castleton Manor," Faith said. "But I gave it to the police. It's evidence in the investigation of Oscar North's death."

Burke's smile thinned even more. "That is most unfortunate."

"Did you give the token to Oscar North?"

The man's smile disappeared entirely.

The hair rose on the back of Faith's neck. She thought again of lightning and how people's hair stood up just before they were struck.

"I'm not in the habit of being questioned," Burke said quietly.

Faith hugged Watson tighter as she wondered if there was any chance she could run back to the library without Burke catching her.

She discarded the idea. Really, her only way out was to plunge ahead, so she decided her best option was not to show fear. Burke seemed like a man who responded aggressively to fear.

She narrowed her eyes at him. "You might have a chance to get more in the habit," she said, trying to match Burke's quiet aggression. "The police are quite interested in the origin of the chip." Of course, that was a lie as far as she knew. Officer Tobin certainly hadn't shown much interest in it.

They stared at each other in silence for a moment.

Then, to Faith's surprise, he said, "Fine. I gave Oscar North the chip to let him know he needed to pay his debt."

"Oscar owed you money?"

Burke nodded. "A great deal of money. He thought he was a gambler, but he was mostly an ATM, up until he wasn't. He wrote a few IOUs, but he seemed to forget the *owe* part."

"The police might see that as a motive for murder."

Burke barked out a harsh laugh. "Then they'd be stupid. Dead men rarely pay their debts, so they don't have much value for me. The worst that would have happened to North would have been a bit of vandalism of his nice house. Maybe a tiny scare for the wife. But it hadn't come to that. North promised to pay, and he had started doing so. It wasn't as fast as I would have liked, but he was paying."

"So you had no reason to kill him," Faith stated. She tended to doubt most of what the man said, but she didn't think it would be wise to push him any further.

"I'm not a violent man. I'm a businessman." Then Burke smiled again. It wasn't any nicer than the earlier one. "And I like to keep my business quiet, so I'd rather you didn't tell the police about our little chat."

Fear stole Faith's voice, and she didn't respond right away.

Burke clearly read her expression. "You can relax, Miss Newberry. I'm not going to hurt you either way. It does nothing good for my business if I go around hurting cat ladies."

Faith found that she actually believed him. But even if Burke hadn't intentionally murdered Oscar North, that didn't mean he hadn't sent someone to the manor to scare the man, someone who might have chased Oscar onto the balcony. Oscar could have easily climbed the railing, thinking to jump down and get away, never expecting to fall to his death instead.

"You know, whoever killed Oscar might not have meant for him to die," she said. "If someone was trying to scare him into doing something, they might have scared him right off that balcony."

Burke laughed again. "You have a vivid imagination. It must be from all the book reading. I had no idea Oscar was at Castleton Manor. I didn't track the man's movements. Like I said, he was paying. I only heard about the blackbird chip and came to ask for its return."

"You heard about the chip but not about where Oscar was?" Faith said.

"I have many friends who watch out for my interests with much enthusiasm," Burke told her. "They tell me things, but I have no control over which things. But none of them have told me of killing Oscar."

Faith suspected Burke would cheerfully lie about the activities of those friends. But it did bring up another possibility. What if one of these friends had decided to retrieve the blackbird chip for Burke by stealing her purse? The man standing in the pool of light could be indirectly responsible for Watson's injury. The thought brought a fierce flare of anger, but Faith had no idea what to do with it. Burke would only lie if she asked him about it.

"I need to go," she said, well aware that her anger colored her voice. "I have an appointment at the police station. I don't want them to have to come searching for me. They're very conscientious here."

"So I've heard." The man tipped his head toward her. "Good night, Miss Newberry. This has been interesting. Do keep an eye on your cat. Cats are always so curious. And you know what curiosity did to the cat." Leaving a vague air of menace, he slid back into the shadows and strode away.

Faith gulped a few calming breaths of air, then hurried to the safety of her SUV. She didn't begin to feel safe again until she pulled into a parking space in front of the police station.

It took some insistence to bring Watson with her to see Officer Tobin, but she wasn't about to leave the cat alone and vulnerable in her vehicle, even if the heat of the day had cooled with the darkness.

When she finally reached Officer Tobin, she spilled the whole parking lot encounter with Michael Burke while holding Watson close to her chest. She knew it probably made her look like the crazy cat lady that Burke had implied she was, but she didn't care.

As she spoke, Officer Tobin's face darkened more and more. "Did Burke threaten you in any way?" he asked. "I won't have some thug terrorizing citizens in Lighthouse Bay, and I know the chief feels the same way. I don't care how much money Burke has."

"He didn't exactly threaten me." Faith repeated the man's remark about curiosity and cats.

"I'm glad you told me about this," Tobin said, then gave her an approving smile. "He didn't know what tough stuff you and Watson are made of."

"I didn't feel tough. You know, I wonder now if my purse being stolen might be connected to Burke. He admitted that he wanted the blackbird chip, and he thought I had it. He didn't take responsibility for what happened to me, but he did hint that someone might do things for him."

"That chip is linked to an illegal, high-stakes gambling house. It moves around, and we haven't been able to bust it, but knowing the chip is definitely tied to Burke should be helpful. We've suspected him, but we've had to split our manpower between several possible suspects. Now we can focus on property connected to Burke."

"In that case, it seems odd that he'd approach me," Faith said.

Tobin smiled again. "I suspect he thought we already knew. Sometimes the bad guys assume we have more information than we do.

We'd have gotten there eventually, but this will move things along." Then the smile vanished as his expression clouded with worry. "It's possible Mr. North could have been considering coming to us. A witness to the actual operation would have been invaluable. We could have arrested Burke. Something like that could get a man killed."

"None of this is going to make me sleep any easier tonight," Faith said.

"I hate to say it, but it shouldn't." Tobin frowned at her. "You need to be careful, and you need to leave this investigation alone."

"I want to leave it alone," she insisted, "but it keeps coming to me."

"Then you might want to think about a little time away. Maybe visit some family. Honestly, you don't want to mess with Burke. He's a loose cannon."

As Faith had predicted to Officer Tobin, the events of the evening didn't help her sleep. She woke several times in the night and wandered through the cottage, making sure the doors and windows were locked. Each time, Watson stirred and grumbled in protest.

Finally, morning sun met her when she jerked away from another disturbing dream, and Faith was glad to put the night behind her. She showered and slipped into a blue cotton dress, hoping the cheerful color would distract from the dark circles her makeup didn't quite disguise. She packed spare clothes for riding with Wolfe later and headed for work with Watson trotting along at her heels. She didn't feel comfortable leaving him behind at home after the veiled threats of the night before.

As soon as Faith and Watson stepped into the sunny foyer of the manor, she spotted Nina in an intense discussion with Marlene. The two women looked much alike as they stood practically nose to nose.

Nina caught sight of Faith and marched over to her. "You must do something. Please."

Marlene followed. "This is hardly a matter for our librarian," she said, putting a less than complimentary emphasis on the word *librarian*.

Nina ignored her. "It's Benjamin. He never came back to his room. He's been missing for a day at least."

"As I told you, Miss Borz," Marlene said loudly, "guests are free to come and go as they wish. Mr. Mace may have stayed a night in Lighthouse Bay. Or gone to visit friends. Or met a new friend."

"He did none of those things," Nina snapped at her. She turned back to Faith. "Benjamin couldn't have left of his own volition. Something has happened. Something horrible."

Faith glanced at Marlene. "It does sound like we should look for him."

Marlene's expression turned even more sour. "Really? Is that what you intend to do with your day instead of your librarian duties? Our staff members are busy enough as it is."

Faith nodded. "You're right, but I wonder if Mr. Jaxon might still consider hiring some extra people. They could help with the search. I'll be seeing him later. I could ask."

Marlene practically turned green at that suggestion.

But Faith was honestly becoming worried. Was it possible that the man who had killed Oscar had hung around the manor to make sure no one blamed him before he left? Benjamin had obviously been poking around. If he'd confronted the killer, he could be in trouble. Of course, another possibility was that Benjamin *was* the killer, and he'd made a run for it. Faith hadn't forgotten the man had a motive after being the victim of one of Oscar's cruel gags.

Marlene crossed her arms over her chest. "I suppose we could call Mr. Mace's room."

"I tried that," Nina said, her voice nearly a shriek. "I have called his room. I have called his cell. I have knocked on his door. No answer."

"Perhaps someone should check his room," Faith said to Marlene. "For his own safety. He could have had a medical issue and be in need of assistance while we fuss in the foyer."

Marlene rolled her eyes, then grabbed the key ring at her waist. She removed a key from it and handed it to Faith. "Here's my master. I have real work to do, but clearly you feel you have plenty of spare time. You go check on the room, but then I expect you to open the library. After all, we are a literary retreat. The library should be accessible."

"I'll take care of it." Faith managed not to stomp as she headed for the staircase.

Both Watson and Nina trailed along behind her.

"Thank you, Miss Newberry," Nina said. "I'm glad someone around here cares."

"We all care," Faith said. "But Ms. Russell has protocols she has to follow. Still, I believe we're going to find Mr. Mace."

Nina hurried into the lead since she was the one who knew which room belonged to Benjamin. It turned out to be one of the smaller suites located not far from the balcony.

When they reached the door, Faith knocked sharply.

"That won't work," Nina insisted. "I've knocked until my knuckles are bruised."

"Mr. Mace," Faith called through the door, then tried to listen, but it wasn't easy with Nina chattering beside her. She knocked again, and it was soon evident that no one was going to answer. She slipped the master key into the lock and opened the door.

The room was large and comfortable with dark wood furniture and a masculine air. It was currently messy but not alarmingly so. They found clothes still hanging in the closet, and Benjamin's suitcase was open on a small table. It did not appear the man had left to stay somewhere else.

"See?" Nina said. "He didn't leave. I told you he didn't. So where is he? Where is Benjamin?"

Faith had to admit that was an excellent question. She promised Nina that she would see that a search began.

The other woman nodded and thanked Faith before hurrying out the door.

Faith checked to make sure Watson was safely beside her in the hall and carefully locked the door behind them.

One of the housekeepers rolled a cart toward her. "Can I clean now?"

"You probably shouldn't," Faith said. "Mr. Mace is missing. Until we find him, I'd rather his room stayed as is." Then she had a thought, something she'd intended to handle before. "Do you clean the Jane Austen Suite?"

The young woman nodded, and then her expression turned concerned. "Has someone complained? I reported the broken table leg. That was not my doing. I found it that way."

"It's all right. The guest told me about the table. He tripped and fell on it. When did you first notice the damage?"

The housekeeper's expression grew more alarmed. "Yesterday. I saw the table leg was cracked yesterday morning when I cleaned. I reported it right away."

"It sounds like you handled it correctly." Faith felt bad for worrying the housekeeper, so she gave her what she hoped was a comforting smile. She noticed Watson did his part as well, rubbing against the housekeeper's ankles.

The woman glanced down at Watson and smiled slightly, then looked back at Faith with worried eyes. "I should get going. I still have more rooms to clean."

"Of course. Thank you for talking to me." Faith headed for the stairs with Watson at her heels. She wondered what she'd accomplished other than scaring the housekeeper. She had proved Jordan told the truth about his table, but Jordan hardly seemed like a man who would grab purses to protect Michael Burke. However, Faith would never have pegged Oscar for a man with a gambling problem, so it was possible she was not the best judge of character. Or Louellyn was right—everyone had a mask.

She found several guests chatting beside the statue of Agatha Christie while waiting for the library to open. She apologized profusely and let them in.

The morning passed swiftly as a few guests returned books they'd checked out and others got new ones. To Faith's surprise, not every book checked out was a mystery. Despite their passion for noir, a few guests seemed to prefer biographies, and one older woman was passionate about true crime.

"I've found the real world is as dark and gritty as anything Raymond Chandler wrote," the woman said as she clutched a copy of *The Devil in the White City*.

Faith found such books depressing, but she would hardly tell a guest that, so she merely wished the woman good reading.

She stayed busy until the usual lunch lull. Few people could resist the siren call of the delectable meals Castleton Manor served. Faith was excited at the thought of the afternoon off. After riding with Wolfe, she'd pop back into the library to pick up Watson before heading home.

"I'm happy that you'll be in here," she told the cat as she scratched behind his ears.

Watson blinked sleepy eyes at her, as if in total agreement.

Faith locked the library's main doors that led out onto the gallery and the doors leading to the terrace as well, then ducked into the nearest restroom and changed into jeans and a lightweight blouse. She also swapped out her low-heeled pumps for sneakers. She folded her dress neatly and tucked it into the tote. She'd leave it in the library as well.

She had just stowed the tote bag under her desk when she heard a familiar deep voice from overhead. "Have you had lunch?"

Faith glanced up to see Wolfe, unusually informal in jeans and a blue polo shirt. She smiled at him. "Is sneaking up on me from above going to become a regular thing?"

Wolfe laughed. "Not at all. I didn't want to walk through the gallery in casual clothes. I won't come this way again." He raised a hand. "Scout's honor."

"Thank you," Faith said. "As for lunch, I haven't eaten yet. I only just locked the library."

"Good. I had the kitchen pack a picnic and deliver it to the stable, and I know the perfect spot for us to eat." Wolfe rubbed his hands together. "This will be fun." He nodded toward the cat curled up on Faith's chair. "Is Watson coming?"

"No, I think he'd best stay here out of trouble." She pointed toward the spiral stairs. "Shall I meet you there, or are we going out from the terrace?"

"I'll come down."

Faith was glad that Watson slept through their quiet exit. She always felt a twinge of guilt when she shut a door in the cat's face.

She and Wolfe walked across the glorious back lawn, and she felt lighter with each step that carried her away from all the stress of the past few days. She considered telling him about her encounter the night before, but she decided against it. She simply didn't want to ruin the light mood. "How has your day been?" she asked instead.

"Busy," Wolfe said. "Every day has been too busy lately."

"Did you hear about Benjamin Mace?"

"The missing guest?" He frowned. "Yes. Marlene told me. She seems certain Mr. Mace's friend is blowing the situation out of proportion."

"Maybe, but it is strange."

"We're checking into it. Now let's spend a few hours not worrying about anything. Horses pick up on emotion, and we'll enjoy the ride more if we just let it all go."

Faith smiled. "That sounds wonderful. I'm so glad we're going for a ride. I can use the break. I really should ride more. The horses here are so beautiful."

"They are, though I'm afraid your mount today is not the loveliest of the bunch," Wolfe said as they approached the stable. "Poor old Dusty. She's a bit of a wallflower."

"Only because people don't have good sense." A man strode out of the stable, leading two horses.

Faith immediately recognized Samuel Peak, the head groom, having met him under far less pleasant circumstances in the past. As usual, Samuel looked and sounded gruff, but Faith knew he had a good heart and a passionate love for the horses.

Wolfe held up both hands. "Remember, I didn't insult the horses."

"And I know you never would," Samuel said. Then he nodded to the Arabian horse on his right and addressed Faith. "Dusty is as gentle a mount as you'd ever want. She'll mind you, whether you want to take it slow or do a bit of galloping."

"I might have to work up to galloping," Faith admitted as she studied the horse. Dusty was a pale buff color, somewhere between gray and tan. But the oddest thing about the horse was her profile. She had an unusual forehead bulge. "I've never seen a forehead quite like that," she remarked.

"That's called a *jibbah*," Samuel said. "It's a common trait in Arabian horses, but Dusty's is extreme, which seems to put people off. Legend says the greater the jibbah, the more blessed the horse."

Faith thought the horse must be very blessed indeed. She regarded the huge animal that Wolfe was now patting. It was a striking black gelding. "I can't believe *he* could ever be a wallflower."

"He's not," Wolfe said. "He's a beast."

"We don't let the guests ride Nightstorm," Samuel said, shaking his head. "We'd never be able to afford the insurance."

Wolfe laughed. "He's not so bad. You just have to know how to win him over." With that he took a sugar cube from his pocket and fed it to the snorting horse. "This beast is extremely open to bribery."

"I didn't think to bring you a present," Faith said as she patted Dusty.

"I brought enough to share." Wolfe retrieved another sugar cube from his pocket and handed it to Faith, who gave it to Dusty.

Nightstorm stomped his foot as Dusty munched her treat. Clearly the bigger horse didn't like sharing.

Wolfe and Faith saddled up and headed away from the stable. Faith found that Dusty followed Nightstorm with enthusiasm, requiring little effort from the rider. That suited Faith just fine because it allowed her to enjoy the lovely scenery.

The ground sloped gradually downward, and Faith assumed they were heading for the small beach. Normally the beach was accessed by a much steeper and more treacherous trail, so Faith was glad Wolfe knew a less terrifying route.

Wolfe turned his horse and circled around to ride beside her, leaving enough room so Nightstorm wouldn't be able to nip at Dusty. "Are you having a good time?" he asked.

"I am. It's nice to be outside. The weather is gorgeous."

He nodded. "I love my job, but if I'm not careful, I can forget what sunlight feels like."

Faith motioned toward his horse. "So did you name him Nightstorm?"

"No, he had the name when we bought him. I think he must have been named by a teenager with visions of superheroes." Wolfe smiled. "Unfortunately, the name had already gone to the horse's head, and no one could ride him. It took months for me to convince him that I wasn't going to give up on him."

"I'm glad you did," Faith said. "He's a magnificent horse."

Wolfe reached forward and patted Nightstorm on the neck. "He's a good horse too. He simply knows his own mind."

Faith turned her attention back to the path ahead. The lawn was slowly giving way to more rocks as they moved closer to the beach. She could hear the waves crashing and smell the salt in the air, though she couldn't see the water yet.

What she did see just ahead was a tall rock, pushing up from the ground like a jagged tooth. To her utter shock, a familiar black-and-white cat sat perched on the very top of the rock, delicately washing one of his paws.

"Watson!" Faith shouted.

The detective cat heard his name over the unpleasant sound of a ridiculous amount of water pounding the land not far from where he sat. The cat could feel the rumble of the surf. If given a choice, he wouldn't get any closer to it, but sometimes a sleuth has to face even something as disgusting as water. Nothing kept a detective from his job. It was part of the code.

The cat made sure the glance he gave the horses was nonchalant. It wouldn't do for his human to think he was bothered by the dangerous thing she was doing. Why would she possibly want to climb on such a stinky animal? The cat would never understand humans. That was certain.

Standing to stretch in the most leisurely way possible, the cat turned another glance toward the horses. They were close enough. With a bored yawn, the cat jumped down from the rocks. It was time to lead his human to the next clue, a grisly one. She would never find it on her own.

"Watson!"

The cat ignored her strident tone. She would follow. He knew that from experience. With proper encouragement, his human would follow him anywhere.

The cat hopped from stone to stone until he reached the sandy pit behind the rock outcropping. The pit held more than sand, and the cat sat delicately near the sad contents.

His human stomped around the rocks. "Watson!"

The cat twitched his stub of a tail, waiting for the inevitable praise that was his due. He'd found the biggest clue of all. Surely that discovery had earned him a tunaroon. Or three.

His human froze, her eyes wide and her mouth open as she stared into the pit.

The cat stood, bringing his paw to the spot the human needed to look first.

His human's hand drifted to her face as she staggered toward the pit. For a moment, the cat worried that she might tumble in, and he prepared to jump aside if necessary. But her steps grew less wobbly as she got closer.

The cat stood, ready for the petting.

But his human ignored him and yelled, "Wolfe, come quick! It's Benjamin Mace! I think he's dead!"

13

Faith held Watson close to her chest as she stood beside Wolfe and watched the police process the scene, though she stood back far enough that she couldn't see Benjamin Mace's body. "He seemed like such an inoffensive man," Faith said quietly. "Why would anyone want to kill him?"

"That's just the question we'd like answered," Chief Andy Garris said as he walked over to join them. He removed a clean white handkerchief from his pocket and used it to wipe sweat from his bald head. Then he turned to Wolfe. "Had you met the victim as well?"

"Yes, I spoke to him briefly. It was right before I urged the guests to focus on the retreat and stop their investigation."

"Investigation?" Garris pulled out a notepad and a pen.

"We're holding a literary retreat for noir fiction enthusiasts," Wolfe said. "Some of them seemed to view the death of Oscar North as an invitation to ply the trade they enjoy reading about."

"So you believe the deaths of Oscar North and Benjamin Mace are linked?" the chief asked.

Wolfe glanced at the small swarm of police officers around the rocks. "I don't know."

"How about you, Miss Newberry?" Garris asked. "You're awfully quiet. Do you have any input? Usually you're full of ideas."

Even though the chief's tone had an edge to it, Faith didn't take offense. She knew how much Chief Garris hated seeing violence mar the town he'd sworn to protect. He took his job seriously, and the death of the would-be investigator was nearly as upsetting to the chief as it was to Faith.

"As Mr. Jaxon said, Benjamin Mace was part of the noir retreat,"

Faith said. "On the morning after Oscar North's death, I heard Mr. Mace announce to the widow that he would find out what happened to her husband. He saw himself as a hard-boiled detective, but he didn't seem like a hard man." Then she winced. "And he has a friend who is going to be devastated."

Chief Garris raised his eyebrows. "I'll need the friend's name."

"Nina Borz."

The chief jotted down notes. "Is she a guest at Castleton too?"

Faith nodded. "I talked to her this morning. She was worried because she couldn't find Mr. Mace."

"They were romantically linked?"

"I believe so—in her mind, anyway. I'm not sure if they were actually dating. In fact, I think he might have been avoiding her when he was doing his investigating."

"So she wouldn't know what he might have found that someone would kill over?" Garris asked.

"I'm not sure, but I doubt it," Faith replied. "As far as I know, he wasn't a particularly good private eye. The only clue that I'd heard him find was a fraternity pin, and technically Watson found that."

At the mention of the cat, the chief's expression finally softened, and he reached out to rub Watson's ears. "We could all take some clue-finding lessons from Watson," he said. Then he asked Faith, "Do you know if Mr. Mace still has this fraternity pin?"

"He never had it. Watson brought it to me, and I gave it to Officer Tobin last night."

Garris nodded. "I heard you'd visited the station after your encounter with Michael Burke. I hope Officer Tobin impressed on you the importance of avoiding that man."

Wolfe stirred beside her. "I didn't hear about that. Who is Michael Burke?"

"A local *businessman*." The look of distaste on the chief's face as he said the word made plain his feelings about the man. "He has ties to illegal gambling, and he's obviously becoming bolder about them, considering his accosting Miss Newberry in a public parking lot."

Wolfe turned to Faith with real concern. "Are you all right?"

"Of course." Faith felt her cheeks warm as Wolfe gave her his full attention. She hoped she wasn't turning cherry red in front of him. "I would have told you about it, but it was so nice to go riding and not think about any of the awful things that have happened in the last few days."

"I would rather know, especially if a criminal is harassing you." Wolfe paused, then added, "Or any of my employees."

"Well, I'm fine. I promise," Faith insisted. "Burke only wanted the blackbird gambling chip that Watson found."

"Blackbird?" Wolfe repeated. "I feel like I've been out of the loop. I hope you'll catch me up."

"It might be worthwhile if we *all* compare notes," Garris said.

While Faith was listing the events of the last few days, whether they seemed directly related or not, she was aware of the increasing concern on Wolfe's face. Watson squirmed in her arms, and she was so focused on her employer's darkening expression that she barely noticed when the cat freed himself and jumped down to the sand.

Faith spotted Watson as he darted over to the busy technicians.

"Can someone get this cat?" one of the technicians complained, trying to shoo him away. "He'll contaminate the evidence."

"He was already over there once," the chief said as he turned toward the rocks. "So I don't know how much more contamination he's likely to do."

Watson slipped by the tech and settled on Benjamin Mace's forearm. The cat immediately batted at the man's closed fist.

"Chief!" the tech yelled, picking up the cat.

Faith rushed over and took Watson from the man. "I'm so sorry," she said. "But there must be something in Mr. Mace's hand for Watson to have that kind of interest."

Garris and Wolfe joined them.

"You'd better see what it is," the chief told the tech.

The technician was clearly annoyed, but he bent over Benjamin's arm and gently pried his fingers open. In the palm of his hand lay a small button. "I guess there was something." The man used tweezers to lift the button from Benjamin's hand.

"Let me see." The chief held out a gloved hand, and the tech dropped the button into it. Garris showed it to Faith and Wolfe. "Don't touch it. Is it familiar to either of you?"

"It looks like a button from the cuff of a shirt," Wolfe said. "I think the emblem on it is for a fraternity, but it's not mine."

"Yes," Faith said. "I think it matches the emblem on the fraternity pin Watson found on the balcony at Castleton. It might have belonged to Oscar."

"Oscar North was in a fraternity?" Garris asked.

"I don't think so, but he worked for them at one time as a caterer or some such. His wife told me he had a collection of fraternity pins from every fraternity he ever served," Faith explained. "Maybe all of this is tied to that time in Oscar's life."

The chief turned around and bellowed for Officer Tobin, who stood near the police cars.

The officer stopped writing furiously on some papers on a clipboard, tossed the clipboard into one of the cars, and jogged over to the chief. "You need me, sir?"

Garris held out the button. "Is this the same emblem that's on the fraternity pin Miss Newberry gave you?"

Tobin squinted at it. "Maybe. I'd have to examine them together, but it's weird about the frat pin."

"Weird how?" the chief asked.

"Yesterday before Miss Newberry even dropped the pin off, Mr. Mace came by the station. He wanted to see the pin. I told him we can't show evidence to private citizens, not even if they're wearing a trench coat and a fedora."

Garris gave him a pained expression. "I hope you didn't actually add the part about the trench coat and fedora."

"Of course not," the officer said, but Faith could see him smothering a grin. "At any rate, Mr. Mace stomped off."

"Why didn't you tell me when I came to the station last night?" Faith asked.

"Same problem. I can't share things with private citizens, not even the ones I like. Plus, I didn't think of it since the information about Michael Burke was so much bigger." Tobin cast a rueful glance toward Benjamin's body. "Or I thought so at the time."

Watson started to wriggle in Faith's arms again, so she said, "If you don't need me anymore, Chief, I should probably get back to the manor. Marlene wants me to help with the locked-room activity tonight."

"Marlene can handle the activity on her own," Wolfe said firmly. "You should go home. You've had a terrible shock. Chief, could one of your officers possibly give Miss Newberry a ride to her cottage?"

"Don't you need me to get Dusty back to the stable?" she asked.

Wolfe shook his head. "As long as I'm on Nightstorm, Dusty will follow. I suspect she'd follow him anywhere."

The chief pointed at Officer Tobin. "Give Miss Newberry a lift back to Castleton, and see if you can round up Nina Borz. I'll want to talk to her."

"Do you want me to bring her back here?" Officer Tobin asked.

"No," Garris said. "If she really cared about the guy, she doesn't need to see this. I'll talk to her at the manor. Just track her down for me."

Officer Tobin nodded. He turned toward Faith, bowed slightly, and waved an arm toward the group of police cars. "Your ride awaits."

"And I appreciate it."

Once in the car, Watson settled down to rest quietly in her lap, so she leaned back against the headrest and closed her eyes. The horseback riding had been nice. She thought wistfully of the feeling of being free from all the tension at the manor. Now she was heading back into it, but at least she wouldn't be staying.

"Do you want me to drop you at the cottage?" Officer Tobin asked.

Faith opened her eyes. "No thank you. I need to pick up my stuff from the manor. I had planned to return to the library after horseback riding."

"I haven't been riding in years," Tobin said. "I used to like it. I bet the manor has some fantastic horses."

"They are gorgeous, and Samuel does a great job with them."

He glanced over at her. "That's a rotten way to end your outing. Are you okay?"

"I'll be fine," she said, wondering why people kept asking her that. She thought she must look as shocked and exhausted as she felt. "But I think Watson and I are ready for a quiet evening at home."

"Why don't you grab your stuff at the library and let me drive you to the cottage," Tobin suggested. "I don't want to leave you to walk home alone."

Faith forced a light laugh. "It's not even close to dark, and the gardens are going to be full of guests. I'll be fine walking home. I do appreciate your concern, but I'm not afraid."

"Sometimes you're too brave for your own good." The officer reached into his shirt pocket and pulled out a business card and scrawled something on it. He handed it over to Faith. "That's my cell number."

Faith took the card with a smile. "You've given me your card before."

"I know, but I want it to be easy for you to find. When you get to your house, text me right away so I know you got there safely. I'll feel better."

"Sure, though I'm positive you don't need to worry."

They arrived at the manor bare minutes later, and Faith managed to slip into the library without having to talk to anyone. She was starting to feel increasingly shaken, and she just wanted to get home. She grabbed her purse and her bag of clothes, then locked the library door behind her.

There were plenty of people in the garden, but no one stopped her to talk as she strode purposefully home with Watson in her arms.

She'd learned years before that the easiest way to keep most people from stopping you to chat was to seem intent on getting somewhere.

She wound through the paths of the Victorian garden. It featured a number of heritage breeds of flowers and had a lush, slightly overgrown appearance that mixed with the wrought iron benches. Scattered Victorian sculptures gave it an old and slightly mysterious quality. Faith normally loved the garden, but today it only made her aware of how much the overgrowth blocked visibility. She listened for guest voices, but the garden was quiet.

To her dismay, Watson squirmed out of her arms once more and bounded ahead.

"Don't get lost," she called after him. "I won't go searching for you."

Still, she picked up her pace. She assumed Watson was heading for home, where he stood a good chance of getting a snack, but she couldn't shake off the memory of the purse thief rushing out of the shadows of her cottage entryway. Of course, it was only late afternoon now. The sun was bright, and there weren't many shadows. No one would be sneaking up on her.

Faith finally stepped free of the Victorian garden. She could see the cottage. She was nearly home.

Then someone grabbed her arm.

Faith screamed.

14

A shriek responded to Faith's scream, and her arm was released instantly.

Faith jumped back, turning to see Brooke also staggering backward.

Brooke had a basket on her arm and her other hand on her chest. "You nearly gave me a heart attack," she announced.

"Me?" Faith said. "I'm not the one who snuck up and grabbed me." She wondered how many shocks her heart could take.

"I wasn't sneaking. I was waiting for you." Brooke pointed ahead where the shadow from a dip in the ground partially hid a hole.

When she peered closer, Faith could just make out the scatter of soil around the hole.

"I didn't want you to fall in and get hurt," Brooke continued. "I guess the gardeners went home before they actually planted that bush."

Faith noticed a hydrangea shrub in a large pot sitting a little way from the hole. Beside the shrub were some other tools. "That's strange. The gardeners are normally more careful."

"The staff is plain jumpy," Brooke said. "We've had an unusual number of mishaps in the kitchen too. It doesn't help that your purse was stolen on Castleton property. Half my kitchen assistants expect to be either mugged or murdered by the end of this retreat."

"I don't think anyone is going around randomly attacking people," Faith responded.

"Do you want to help me move the shrub to the hole?" Brooke asked. "It looks like a good way for a guest to fall and break an ankle. I'm afraid someone will think it's a shadow and end up suing the manor for an injury."

Faith nodded and followed Brooke over to the hydrangea shrub in the big pot. Brooke set her basket down. The pot was heavier than it appeared, and it took both of them to haul it closer to the hole.

As soon as they had it in place, Faith dusted her hands off on her jeans. "So you came all the way out here to warn me about the gardeners?"

Brooke motioned toward her basket. "No, I came all the way out here to bring you supper. I have the night off, and I want to hear all about your date with Wolfe. I am a woman in dire need of happy stories of romance." Her eyes sparkled as she added, "I even brought you a box of strawberry thumbprint cookies, made with jam from Eileen's recipe."

At the thought of food, Faith's stomach growled. She and Wolfe had missed out on the picnic lunch and had stood around for hours with the police. Now she was starving. "Thanks for bringing dinner. You're a lifesaver."

Watson galloped over to them as if he'd overheard their conversation about food. He rubbed against Brooke's ankles, purring loudly.

Brooke bent down to scratch behind Watson's ears, then collected her basket.

Faith linked her arm through Brooke's and towed her toward the cottage. "I'm afraid I won't be able to feed your romance fantasies. But I'll tell you all about what happened, even though I wasn't on a date and it had the most unromantic ending in the history of outings."

"How could it not have been romantic? Did Wolfe sneeze on you when he went in for the kiss?" Brooke teased.

"First, there was no attempted kissing, and second, Watson showed up." Faith glanced down at the cat trotting beside her.

"And you two couldn't just ignore him?" Brooke scoffed. "We need to up your romance game."

"We couldn't ignore him. Watson discovered a dead body not far from the beach."

"A dead body!" Brooke yelped. "Now you *really* have to tell me all about it as soon as we get inside." She tugged Faith across the lawn to the front door.

As soon as Faith unlocked the door, Watson scampered ahead of them into the kitchen. She filled his dishes, and he ate hungrily.

Brooke made Faith sit down at the table while she put out the food. She'd made wraps stuffed with the lemon-and-herb chicken the manor was serving for dinner as well as crisp vegetables straight from the garden. She'd also brought a glass jug of fresh lemonade, and for dessert she had fruit hand pies in addition to the cookies.

"I'm a terrible hostess," Faith said as she watched her friend bustle around the cozy kitchen. "You're doing all the work."

Brooke poured a glass of lemonade. "You're a wonderful hostess who has had a hard day, and I'm glad to help." She handed Faith the glass. "The body didn't belong to anyone we know, did it? Please tell me that my kitchen staff isn't right that someone is stalking Castleton Manor with murder and mayhem in mind."

"It wasn't staff, so I don't know if you met him." Faith stared glumly into her glass. "It was a guest. Benjamin Mace. He was one of those who always wore a trench coat."

Then she froze, remembering that the body they'd found had been missing the trench coat. Benjamin had worn the coat every other time Faith had seen him, even out on the balcony where the heat certainly couldn't have made it pleasant. Of course, the trek to the rocks was a lengthy one, and most likely he'd simply decided not to wear the coat. Faith wondered if the coat was in his room.

"I can see those gears turning," Brooke said as she set her own glass of lemonade on the table and slid into the chair across from Faith. "What?"

"Nothing really. I just realized Benjamin wasn't wearing his trench coat."

"I can't imagine anyone wanting to wear a coat all the way to the beach. The breeze off the water is nice, but it *is* still summer."

Faith nodded and took a sip of her lemonade. It was sweet and tangy and cold, the perfect combination. She set it carefully back on the table. After the shocks of the last days, she felt the need to do everything carefully, as if moving too fast might make her break down.

"It's more than Benjamin that's bothering you," Brooke said, studying her.

"It's definitely been a tough few days." Faith picked a bit of cucumber out of her wrap and munched on it. Then she caught Brooke up on the confrontation with Michael Burke and the things the police had said about him.

Brooke leaned partway across the table, her blue eyes wide. "That definitely sounds scary. Do you think Michael Burke killed Oscar and Benjamin?"

"I don't know what to believe. Burke said he wanted Oscar alive so he could pay his debt. And it does sound like Oscar was trying to do just that since he must have been funneling money out of the restaurant to pay for his gambling habit."

Brooke settled back and picked up her wrap. "That wouldn't have made his wife too happy."

"I don't think it made her upset enough to kill him, if she even knew about it. She seemed genuinely distraught over his death." Faith took a nibble of her wrap. It was as scrumptious as she'd expected.

Brooke chewed her bite slowly, then spoke up again. "The balcony isn't that high. Maybe no one intended to kill Oscar, and that's why the wife was distraught. She killed him, but she didn't mean to."

"But she was at my opening lecture." Faith shook her head. "I don't think she did it."

Brooke gestured at her with the wrap in her hand. "Not to dig up old news, but you tend to think the best of people. It's not like you haven't befriended killers before."

"Thanks." Faith set the wrap back on the plate. "If I was going to point at anyone connected with the restaurant, it wouldn't be Louellyn. It would be Preston Barnwell. He was Oscar's business partner so he was suffering financially from the losses. Plus, his interest in Louellyn seems like more than friendly support to me."

Brooke whistled softly. "The whole thing is so complicated."

Watson meowed as if in agreement.

Brooke glanced at the floor where the cat was staring at both of them. She picked a piece of chicken out of her wrap and tossed it to him, then shot a guilty look at Faith. "Sorry. I couldn't help it. He was watching us with such hope-filled eyes."

Faith laughed. "Well, I hope Watson can keep himself out of trouble from now on. I would honestly like to stay out of this mess for the rest of the retreat. The police are far better equipped to handle it."

"You really think you'll have that option?" Brooke asked.

"Sure," Faith said, then felt a pang of guilt at the lie. She was almost positive the whole business wasn't done with her yet.

Faith's feeling of impending doom followed her through the evening and chased her through her dreams.

The next morning, she again counted on makeup to hide the dark circles under her eyes.

"You don't have to follow so close," she told Watson as she gathered her things to head to work. "I wasn't going to leave you behind. At the rate you're finding all the clues, someone might come after you here."

Watson's meow sounded almost smug, but then most of his meowing did. Faith suspected her cat had a rather positive self-image.

Almost as an afterthought, Faith grabbed the small box of strawberry thumbprint cookies that Brooke had made for her. At least she'd have a snack to cheer her up during the day.

As she walked through the gardens with Watson at her feet, she wondered who had told Nina about Benjamin's death. The poor woman would certainly be suffering. She thought of how often brokenhearted women figured into noir novels. The theme of this retreat was entirely too appropriate.

When she reached the manor and entered the gallery, she spotted the other brokenhearted woman she'd come into contact with lately. Louellyn stood outside the library, peering through the locked doors at the shadowy interior. The woman wore a slim black dress with shoes to match. A black fascinator with a scrap of veil was pinned to her upswept blonde curls.

"Louellyn," Faith said as soon as she was in hearing range, "are you waiting for me?"

Louellyn turned toward her. She had a healthier color than Faith had seen on her before, and her eyes were no longer red. Evidently the widow was beginning to find her footing in the grief over her husband. "I had to find out if the rumor was true. Did someone else die from a fall?"

"There has been another death," Faith agreed gently. "But I don't know the cause, and the police are still investigating."

"Do you know who it was?"

"A guest from the retreat."

Louellyn put her hand to her chest and took a couple of deep breaths. "Do you think there's a serial killer?"

"I'm sure there isn't." Faith gestured toward the library doors. "How about I let us in, and we can sit and talk comfortably." She knew Marlene would go ballistic if she heard someone discussing a Castleton Manor serial killer in the gallery.

Once they were in the library, Faith led Louellyn to one of the chairs near the fireplace.

Watson joined them and perched on a low table, where he seemed to study Louellyn.

"Can I get you something?" Faith asked her.

Louellyn shook her head. "I just wanted to know if Oscar's death is part of a pattern. I'm wondering if it has more to do with the manor than . . . anything else."

"I don't know that the two deaths are connected at all," Faith said, though she suspected they were. "Like I said, the police are investigating. I'm sure they'll work it out."

"You certainly have a lot of confidence in the police force." Louellyn's tone was sharp, almost snippy.

"I've had plenty of reasons to develop a respect for local law enforcement," Faith replied. She really wanted to change the subject, so she asked, "Did you happen to examine Oscar's pin collection?"

Louellyn's expression turned blank. "Pin collection?"

"The fraternity pins? You were going to see if the pin I found came from his collection. If it might be missing a pin."

"Oh, right." Louellyn folded her hands in her lap and turned her gaze toward Watson, who stared right back at her. "I forgot all about it, but I don't think I would have been able to tell if a pin was missing. Oscar's organization, even of a collection, was haphazard at best. Honestly, I never understood why he kept the pins in the first place."

"You mentioned his feelings about the job before. Why did he hate it so much?"

"He hated the frat boys."

"Do you know why?"

"He thought they were lazy and pampered. Oscar felt like he was smarter than the whole lot of them, but he was the one working while they looked down on him." Louellyn sighed. "I think that's part of why he liked playing pranks on them. He said they had no sense of humor. It was the jokes that eventually got him fired from that job. I don't know which one specifically, but considering how much he hated those boys, I can't imagine any of his shenanigans were kind."

"So you don't know which frat boy might have been the target of the trick that got him fired?" Faith asked.

Louellyn picked a nearly invisible speck of lint from her dress. "It was all years and years ago, way before I ever met Oscar. Even if the prank was stupid and mean, that would be an awfully long time to hold a grudge."

"It would," Faith said softly. But she'd heard Nina talk about the practical joke against Benjamin Mace and knew grudges could feed themselves over time. Then she thought of the clue found clutched in the dead man's hand. "Do you know if Oscar collected anything from that time other than pins? Clothes maybe? I know frats sometimes wear matching shirts. Or maybe just buttons from clothes?"

Louellyn shook her head. "Oscar wasn't *that* obsessed with the fraternities. I definitely would have wanted answers if he'd been keeping a wardrobe of frat gear."

"Would you do me a favor?" Faith asked. "When you have a chance, would you snap some pictures of Oscar's collection of fraternity pins? You could just e-mail me the pictures." She rattled off her e-mail address connected to the library. "I could give you a card if it would help you remember."

"You'd best do that. My memory hasn't been all that great since . . ." Louellyn allowed her voice to trail off and smoothed the fabric of her dress over her lap. When she met Faith's gaze, her eyes were damp again. "Preston says that's normal. It's part of stress and grief. But I feel like I have half a brain."

"It is normal," Faith assured her. "Let me get you a card." She got up and hurried to her desk to retrieve one of her business cards. She wrote her cell phone number on the back and carried it over. "You can e-mail the photos to this address or text them to me. I put my cell number on the back in case you need anything. Thanks for doing this."

"Anything to help," Louellyn said. "Do you think it will help? Do you think the fraternities are important?"

"They might be," Faith said. *Or they might be a red herring.* She reminded herself that she was smack-dab in the middle of a whole group of people who loved mysteries. Nearly any of them could come up with some good red herrings to distract the police from the real culprit.

Louellyn tucked the card into the small clutch she carried and stood. She smiled at Faith. "I do appreciate how patient you've been with me. I know now that it was inappropriate for me to demand that you find Oscar's killer. I was out of my head over everything."

"It's all right," Faith said. "No apology necessary."

"Thank you." Louellyn strode out of the library, her head high.

Faith considered the things she'd just heard. Two clues related to fraternities had turned up, one for each of the deaths. And now she knew Oscar had hated the fraternity members he served. Did they hate him back? And if so, how much? What exactly would make anyone hold a grudge for so long?

15

After Louellyn left, Faith headed for her desk. She wanted answers, but she didn't believe they were so pressing that she needed to interrupt Eileen at work, so she decided not to call. Instead, she sat down to compose an e-mail asking what Eileen had learned about the fraternity pin Watson had found. That way her aunt could answer when she had some spare minutes.

As soon as she'd sent it, Faith gazed around the library. It was unusual for it to be empty first thing in the morning. She checked the event schedule and noticed that a panel discussion was under way in the music room on mood and music in noir films, and out in the gardens, the head gardener was leading a tour and talking about flowers as symbols in literature. The garden tour was one of the ticketed events open to the public. Between the two, they'd apparently captured all the retreat guests, leaving Faith with a rare moment of quiet.

She decided to take advantage of the lull with a quick trip to the gift shop for a cup of coffee to go with her strawberry thumbprint cookies. She had rushed through her morning coffee and suspected she'd be dragging by lunchtime without the caffeine boost.

"I'm going to see Iris," she told Watson. "You want to come? I might buy you a treat."

At the word *treat*, Watson stopped blinking sleepily and sat up at full attention.

Faith laughed and picked him up. "I thought a treat might interest you."

As she headed off to the gift shop, she saw staff scurrying around and taking advantage of the respite to clean up and run errands. But she didn't spot a single trench coat between the library and the gift shop. She hadn't realized how ubiquitous they'd become until she was able to pass through the halls without catching sight of one.

Iris gave her a bright smile as she walked into the shop. "I've been seeing a lot of you lately. Is my coffee that good?"

"It is," Faith said. "Plus, I appreciate talking to someone who isn't wearing a fedora and a trench coat."

"You just missed Marlene's daily inspection of my displays," she said. "But I don't think her heart was in it today. She barely moved anything."

"Poor Marlene," Faith said. "She must be in a frenzy after yesterday."

"She was certainly distracted," Iris agreed. "I heard you found the body."

"Watson did actually." Faith shuddered. "It was horrible, and I'd love to not think about it, at least not until I get a lot more caffeine."

"One tall coffee, coming up," Iris said. "And since you've brought Watson, I assume he has an order as well."

"Definitely. I mentioned a treat to him in the library. If I left without one, he'd give me the cold shoulder all day."

Watson meowed plaintively.

Faith laughed. "See? The poor guy is clearly starving."

"We can't have that." Iris grinned. "What do you say, Watson? Tunaroon?"

Watson meowed again.

Iris passed the fish-flavored snack to Faith, who put the cat on the floor and gave him the treat. He took it with his usual delicacy.

"Not to bring up the topic of yesterday again, but are you all right?" Iris asked as she handed a cup of coffee to Faith.

"I will be. I knew Mr. Mace. He was a bit gung ho about the detecting, but he didn't seem like someone with enemies." Faith took a sip of her coffee and sighed softly as the warmth spread through her, making her aware of how chilled she'd felt at her core, despite the summer heat outside.

"Are the police sure his death was murder?" Iris asked.

"I don't see how it wouldn't be. It's a long way to walk, and I doubt Mr. Mace just decided to go for a stroll and ended up behind some rocks. The police didn't make any pronouncements about it yesterday. But Wolfe was still at the scene when I left, so he might know more."

Iris raised her eyebrows. "You and Wolfe were there together?"

"Don't say it like that. We were out riding a couple of the manor's horses because they needed the exercise."

"Of course." Iris began wiping the counter in front of her. Her expression was overly innocent. "I'm sure you were only doing your duty as a Castleton employee." Then she looked up, her eyes sparkling. "A duty I wouldn't have minded when I was young and single."

Faith decided to ignore the teasing. She bought a second treat for Watson, and they returned to the library. Since the room was still empty, Faith sat down with her coffee and cookies and checked her e-mail. She was glad to see she'd gotten a response from her aunt.

I'm so sorry. I haven't had much time to research. I found a collector's site with pictures of fraternity pins but some of the photos are terrible, and it's slow going. Plus, Gail and Seth are still out of commission with some dreadful stomach bug. I suppose that's the cost of working with the public. I will spend more time with the site as soon as I have a chance. Until then, you might want to check it out.

Eileen had ended the e-mail with a link to the site.

"Well, I know what I'll be doing after work tonight," Faith said to Watson. "It's going to be a research night."

From the disdain on the cat's face, Faith could almost believe he understood her.

She needed to peruse the list of retreat guests with library books to prepare the reminder notices. In the past, sometimes guests had carried Castleton books home to finish, and Faith was always looking for polite ways to get all the books back to the library by the time everyone left. She had just pulled up the list on the computer when the door to the library opened.

Preston walked in, carrying a book. "I came to return this. I enjoyed it quite a bit."

Faith walked over to take the book from him, surprised by his friendly tone. The last time she'd seen him, he'd been decidedly more aggressive. "I'm so glad. Will you want another book?"

He shook his head. "I picked up a Cass Morton mystery from the gift shop. That sort of story is a bit outside my normal reading, but I thought I would expand my literary horizons. And I hoped she might sign it for me."

"I wouldn't be surprised. She seems very nice."

Preston glanced around the library. His tone cooled a bit as he said, "I hope the police are going to stop hounding Louellyn now. With a second murder, they must know Louellyn isn't involved."

"I honestly have no idea what the police think," Faith admitted. "But I do know Benjamin Mace was trying to find Oscar's killer. He'd made an impassioned promise to Louellyn about it."

Preston's eyes widened. "I hadn't heard that. Well, that explains a lot."

Faith wondered what exactly that explained.

But before she could ask, Preston continued. "I saw him yesterday."

"You saw Mr. Mace?" Faith asked.

Preston nodded. "He was heading toward the beach with a woman. I couldn't tell much about the woman except that she wore a trench coat just like him."

Faith's attention pricked up sharply. "Mr. Mace was wearing his trench coat?"

Preston harrumphed. "It is the uniform of noir events. I must admit I draw the line at courting heatstroke, so I try not to wear one if I'm going outside."

Faith was mildly amused by Preston's position on wearing his trench coat only inside. This retreat was certainly turning things upside down.

"Watching everyone wander around the gardens sweating is the most foolish thing I've ever seen," he went on.

"People enjoy a little playacting sometimes," Faith said, though she'd also thought wearing a trench coat in the summer heat was rather silly. But a question continued to roll around in her head: *What happened to Benjamin's coat?* "The woman who was with Mr. Mace, you couldn't see her at all?"

"Not really. I think she was quite tall. They were walking on uneven ground, so it was difficult to judge their heights." Preston stared at the floor and appeared to study the toes of his shoes.

It seemed like he wanted to say something more, so Faith waited for him to continue.

"To be perfectly honest," Preston said after a moment, "at first I worried that the woman might be Louellyn. I couldn't imagine her being interested in that little man, but if it *was* her, I'm sure she was only answering questions about Oscar's death." He shook his head slowly. "But the more I think about it, the more I'm sure it wasn't her. The woman didn't move like Louellyn, and she was too thin."

"Then what about the woman made you think of Louellyn at the time?" Faith asked. "I hadn't seen her in a trench coat before."

"Blonde hair." Preston finally looked at her. "I thought I saw some blonde hair under the woman's fedora. But it wasn't Louellyn. I'm sure of it. She wouldn't go strolling in that ridiculous outfit."

"It does seem unlikely," Faith said. But it made her wonder if Preston confused a stranger with Louellyn because of his obvious obsession with his partner's wife. Or was he now convincing himself that it wasn't Louellyn because he didn't want her linked to a second murder? And if it was Louellyn, why hadn't she mentioned talking to Benjamin Mace so soon before he died?

As Preston left the library, several other guests came in. Since they were soon followed by several more, Faith assumed the panel discussion and the garden tour had ended. For the rest of the morning, she stayed busy checking in books and talking with guests. Though most of the attendees knew about Benjamin Mace and remarked on his death in whispered tones, none of them seemed to know Faith had been the one who found the body, because they didn't have any questions for her about it.

To Faith's relief, some of the discussion revolved around a topic she was much more comfortable with—books. She was listening to a tiny elderly woman in a pale green trench coat talk about her love of private eye novels when she heard her phone give the soft beep that signaled a text. Then it beeped a few more times. It took all of Faith's willpower not to reach into her pocket to see if the messages were related to the murders.

"I think it's their charisma," the tiny woman said, blinking owlishly at Faith. "Noir detectives are simply so *manly*."

"Except when they're women." This comment came from Cass, who had slipped in with another group of guests.

The elderly lady flapped a hand at Cass. "That's just unnatural. I never read those kinds of books."

"That's too bad," Faith said. "You could be missing out on some interesting stories."

The woman stared at Cass and Faith, then clucked her tongue. "You young people want to change *everything*!" Then she turned and marched away, muttering softly about the absurdity of lady investigators.

"Do you think she gets the irony of wearing a trench coat while disparaging lady detectives?" Cass whispered to Faith.

Faith chuckled. "Other than overhearing painful conversations about your life's work, how are you enjoying the retreat?"

"I think I could get used to all this opulence," Cass said. "But the Dizzy Dame books would have to sell a lot more copies for that. I did want to ask you something. I'm thinking of setting one of the novels in a fancy place like this. Is there any way I could get a behind-the-scenes tour? I'd love to see some of the staff areas so I can get a feel for that for my book."

"I might be able to arrange it. Let me make a call." Faith pulled her phone out of her pocket. The first thing she noticed was that the texts she'd gotten were from Louellyn. She'd sent photos from Oscar's fraternity pin collection. Faith didn't take time to go through them, but she definitely wanted to talk to Louellyn again, and the texts gave her an idea.

First things first, she reminded herself. She decided she wasn't up to chatting with Marlene, who tended to lead with no as the answer to any question. So Faith took a chance and called Wolfe. She knew she'd pay for going over Marlene's head, but some days it was worth the extra crabbiness to postpone a conversation with the assistant manager.

Wolfe sounded genuinely pleased when he answered the phone. "I'm glad you called. I was meaning to get down to the library and see how you were after yesterday."

"I'm fine. Thank you," she said. "I wanted to ask you a favor for a guest. You remember Cass Morton, of course."

"Of course," Wolfe said. "She gave an excellent speech."

"I thought it was excellent too," Faith said, smiling at Cass. "She has stayed over a few days to relax and soak up some Castleton atmosphere for potential use in a future book. She wants to know if she could see any of the staff areas."

"That would be fine," Wolfe said. "Why don't you take her to the kitchen for lunch? I'll call to let them know you're coming, and you can show her around a little downstairs."

"That sounds great. Let me see if she'd like that," Faith said, then passed along the message.

Cass's face lit up. "It sounds fantastic. Exactly what I was hoping for."

Wolfe apparently heard the woman's response because he said, "Very good. I'll make the call. If I can find a minute, I may come down and join you."

"That would be nice," Faith agreed and ended the call.

"Do you think I have time to run up to my room before we go to lunch?" Cass said. "I need to grab a notebook. I'll definitely want to jot down some impressions."

"Absolutely," Faith said. "There's more than an hour until lunch. If you want to meet me here, we'll walk down together."

"That's even better. I can work for a bit and then come down. Thanks for making this happen." The writer hurried out of the library.

Faith smiled. At least she'd made one person happy. While she had her phone out, she made a quick call to her aunt. "Do you want to go to dinner with me?"

"That sounds wonderful," Eileen said. "Are you bribing me so I'll research that pin? Because I want to do it. It's just crazy here with Seth and Gail out."

"No, I need to do a little research myself. I want to bump into Louellyn and ask her something, and I thought we could go to Driftwood."

"Ah, sneaky. I'm always up for seafood, so you're on. Do you want to meet me here when the library closes?"

"Let's meet at the restaurant. We'll want our own cars anyway."

"It's a date." Eileen suggested a time, and Faith agreed.

As Faith ended the call, another guest walked up with a book in his hands.

"Do you think we should check out early?" the man asked. "It seems like someone is picking off noir enthusiasts, and I have no interest in being killed in my sleep."

The other browsers in the library all perked up at the man's question.

With a sigh, Faith explained that no one was being killed in their sleep, and she was sure they were safe staying until the end of the retreat. Castleton Manor did *not* have a noir serial killer. She was glad to see relief on some patrons' faces, but others didn't seem convinced.

When lunchtime grew close, Faith was relieved to see the library empty of guests. As she gathered a few books to return to their shelves, Watson's loud yowl drew her attention.

He stood at the doors to the terrace and pawed at the glass.

"I'm coming, Rumpy," Faith said, dumping the books on her desk. "If Marlene hears you, you'll end up banned from the library." Not that she had any idea how the assistant manager would enforce a rule like that with Watson's skills at appearing wherever he wanted. She opened the door to the terrace.

Watson raced out, bounded over to the nearest bench, and leaped into the lap of the woman seated there.

Faith recognized Nina, and she rushed out in case the guest didn't appreciate Watson's unusual show of friendliness. She'd barely stepped through the door before Faith realized Nina was crying.

The woman turned a tearstained face toward Faith.

"Miss Borz," Faith said, "are you all right?"

Nina reached out and clutched Faith's arm. "I did it! It's all my fault," she howled. "I killed Benjamin!"

16

Faith slowly settled onto the bench beside the weeping woman. "You killed Benjamin?"

With a hiccuping sob, Nina nodded. "He was my best friend, and I killed him." She dissolved into choked tears.

Faith patted her on the arm gently. "How did you kill Benjamin?"

Nina scrubbed at her face with a handful of tissues. "I didn't mean to. I couldn't have known."

With each answer punctuated by another flurry of sobbing, Faith suspected it was going to take a long time to get any real information from Nina. She wondered if she should simply call the police. She decided to try again. "Miss Borz, you need to calm down. Tell me what happened. Maybe I can help."

Again Nina hiccuped. "Help? How can you help? He's dead." The word *dead* set her off again.

Watson had been sitting quietly in Nina's lap, but Faith could tell by the cat's restless movements that he was getting agitated by the woman's sobbing. She started to reach for him, but she didn't quite make it in time. Nina shifted on the bench, and Watson sank his claws into her leg to avoid falling.

Nina yelped just before Watson jumped down to the tiled terrace. Surprisingly, the pain seemed to distract her from crying. She only sniffled a few times as she rubbed at her legs.

"I'm sorry," Faith said.

Nina gave her a watery smile. "That's okay. You should see the scratches I get from Chandler's nails sometimes." She dabbed at her eyes.

Faith hated to risk sending the woman into a crying frenzy again, but she still couldn't decide on the right response to Nina's apparent revelation. "Miss Borz," she prompted.

"Nina," the woman answered, smiling shakily. "You can call me Nina. You've been so kind."

"Nina," Faith said, "what exactly happened with you and Benjamin?"

Nina blinked at her rapidly for a moment but didn't fall apart. Instead, she cleared her throat and said, "First, I lied to you. I told you I hadn't seen Benjamin at all when I was trying to get you to search for him. Actually, I had. He was heading across the back lawn, and I realized he was ditching me again. I was so angry with him for following his leads in the case without me. I knew he was competitive, but I thought we were *friends*." She stretched the last word out with a wail.

Faith tried to head off another bout of crying by speaking firmly. "Did you ask him about that?"

"Yes, and he said a detective has to move fast. He said that's why it's called 'chasing leads.'" Nina tightened her fist around the wad of tissues. "I was so mad. I told him that he couldn't count on me to have his back anymore. I told him that since he wanted to be alone, he should consider himself alone. Then he died." She burst into tears all over again.

Faith waited quietly until Nina was able to continue.

"It's all my fault for leaving him to face danger without me. I knew he was too brave for his own good. I should have been with him. But my stupid pride got in the way."

"You don't know that it would have helped," Faith said. "You might have been hurt too. Benjamin wouldn't have wanted that."

Nina sniffled, her expression hopeful. "Do you think that was it? He saw how dangerous the case was, and he was trying to protect me?"

Faith suspected Benjamin simply didn't want to share the glory if he solved the case, but she saw no reason to share that with the teary-eyed woman. "It's possible. You knew him better than I did."

Nina nodded vigorously. "He would do something noble like

that. You're right. He was probably trying to keep me safe." Her face brightened as she apparently rewrote the story of her relationship with Benjamin in her head.

"Nina?" Faith said, pulling the woman out of her fantasy. "Did Benjamin tell you where he was going? Did you see?"

"No, and that's part of why I was so angry. He told me he had to meet with a confidential source and I couldn't go along because I might spook the person." Nina huffed in annoyance. "In my normal life I'm a business executive. I know how to handle people."

Faith couldn't believe this nervous, weeping woman in front of her was a business executive. The very idea was almost more than she could process, so she stuck with the topic at hand. "Did Benjamin say if his source was a man or a woman?"

Nina shook her head, but her eyes widened. "You think he might have been meeting with a woman?"

"I honestly don't know. If he did, I'm sure it was directly related to the case."

"But Benjamin was an extremely attractive man," Nina whispered. "Maybe someone used her wiles to get him. I've seen that type in the business world. It happens more often than you'd expect."

"I don't think he would have allowed something like that to distract him from the case," Faith assured her.

"He was focused," Nina agreed. She stood up suddenly. "I should go. I need to check on Chandler. I left him in the suite, and when he gets bored, he can be a bit mischievous."

Faith winced, hoping she didn't mean the little dog might have been destroying Castleton property as they spoke.

Nina walked into the library from the terrace.

Faith stood to follow her in, thinking about what she'd learned. Apparently, the woman Preston saw had been Nina, and that meant Faith didn't need to quiz Louellyn about Benjamin after all.

She considered canceling her dinner with Eileen, but the more she thought about it, the less she liked that idea. She needed some time away from the manor, and she looked forward to talking with her aunt over a nice dinner. With that settled, she scooped Watson up from the terrace railing and headed back inside.

As she walked through the terrace doors, she saw Cass entering the library.

The author chuckled as she approached Faith. "The noir guests are certainly colorful characters. I should be taking notes."

"One lady has a pink trench coat and fedora," Faith said. "And her dog has a matching hat."

Cass laughed. "I like it. Maybe I should give my Dizzy Dame protagonist an outfit like that." She reached out to rub Watson's head. "Are you ready to go? I'm eager to see the mysteries of Castleton."

Faith smiled as she put Watson in one of his favorite napping spots, one of the comfy chairs in front of the fireplace. "I don't have any mysteries to show you, but I can give you a tour of the basement hallways of Castleton."

"I suppose that'll have to do." Cass smiled. "Lead on."

After the wide-open spaces and soaring ceilings of the upstairs levels, the basement hallway felt almost cramped simply by having more normal dimensions. Since the basement was strictly the business area of the manor, the hallway walls were mostly plain, but the well-worn wood floors still glowed with polish. The overall feeling was surprisingly homey and comfortable after the opulence of the guest spaces above.

Most of the basement offices had been servant quarters when Castleton Manor was originally built. Extensive remodeling had combined two or three of the tiny servant rooms to form each office. Faith didn't knock on any of the office doors.

Cass peeked curiously into the bustling laundry as they went by.

Inside, women in neat uniforms carefully folded sheets and towels while chatting amiably. Even though Faith knew the Jaxon family paid well and took good care of their employees, she was always impressed by how cheerful everyone who worked at the manor seemed. Each employee took personal pride in making the manor the best it could be.

The author must have been thinking something similar because she said, "Housekeeping at other places I've stayed is usually much grumpier."

"We have Marlene for that," a young woman whispered as she sailed by, carrying an armload of towels to a waiting cart.

"Marlene?" Cass echoed. "Did she mean Marlene Russell? She does seem to be the odd man out here."

"Ms. Russell is a good manager," Faith said, not wanting to gossip about staff with a guest. "She's extremely detail oriented, and I've never seen such spectacular organizational skills."

Cass grinned. "Which is a diplomatic way of saying she's picky."

Faith suppressed her own smile. "I think they're waiting for us in the kitchen."

As always, the kitchen was busy, but Faith could see Brooke had taken special pains with the table in the back corner. It was draped in a crisp white cloth and even held a vase with a single yellow rose. Two place settings were laid out, and water with lemon waited for them in sparkling crystal glasses.

As soon as she spotted Faith and Cass in the doorway, Brooke rushed over to seat them. "Mr. Jaxon called ahead. And I'm delighted you'll be joining us in the kitchen for lunch. I'm Brooke Milner, the sous-chef here at Castleton Manor."

The author thrust out her hand. "Cass Morton. I've been so impressed by the food during my stay."

Brooke smiled a little shyly as she shook her hand. "I definitely know you, Ms. Morton. I've read every one of the Dizzy Dame novels. They are so fun, and I'm always amazed by how well you hide the killer. I can never guess ahead of time, but when it's revealed, I'm always like, 'Of *course* it was that character!'"

As soon as Brooke released her hand, Cass reached into her bag and pulled out a book. "Do you have this one? It's my newest."

Brooke's eyes widened. "Not yet. I've been waiting for it to come out."

"Let me sign this copy, and you can have it." The author flipped open the book and began writing. "Is that Brooke with an *e* at the end?"

"Yes. This is so nice of you!" Brooke bounced on the balls of her feet as Cass finished the autograph with a flourish.

Cass handed over the book. "I get a lot of free author copies. It's in my contract. I'm always glad to pass them along to fans."

Brooke hugged the book. "Thank you so much. Please have a seat. I'll be serving you. We'll begin with a salad made with greens and veggies from our kitchen garden." She spun and hurried away as Faith and Cass slipped into the chairs.

Cass leaned forward to sniff the rose. "Yellow roses are my favorite."

"Yellow for friendship," Faith said.

Cass sat back. "Back in Victorian times, they stood for infidelity and jealousy."

Faith wrinkled her nose. "That's less cheery."

"A bit. But it was important in one of the Dizzy Dame novels. I love all the symbolism with flowers because it's ambiguous. The message you're sending can be interpreted in so many ways."

"That can happen even when you're just using words." Faith's mind wandered to Benjamin and Nina. She was obviously crazy about him, but she referred to him only as her friend. And Faith doubted he would have used even that word for Nina.

Cass was peering into her face. "Did I lose you there?"

"Sorry. I've had a lot on my mind this week," Faith said. "So, what do you think of your research downstairs?"

"It's disappointing."

"How so? Maybe I can have a word with someone," Faith suggested. *How could Castleton disappoint anyone?*

Cass laughed. "No, nothing like that. It's too clean, bright, and pleasant. I need spooky and dark for my novels. It doesn't look like anything bad could happen here."

Faith thought about the beauty of the terrace outside the library as well as the gorgeous grounds. Bad things had certainly happened in those places. "Unfortunately, bad things don't seem to restrict themselves to dark, scary spots," she mused.

"Even though Castleton appears perfect, this week you're averaging more dead bodies than one of my books," Cass observed.

Faith winced at the blunt remark. "Unfortunately."

"Do you have any ideas about what happened to the victims?" Cass picked up her water glass and took a sip. "Was it murder for sure?"

"I don't think the police have made a decision yet. If they have, they haven't released the information." Faith nearly squirmed, wishing for a change of topic. She tried to steer the conversation back to the reason for this lunch. "I suppose you'll have to use creative license when you write about the staff areas in your book."

"Thankfully, that's a license that I never let expire." With that, their conversation drifted into writing and books, a subject Faith enjoyed much more than murder.

They were deep in a discussion of female protagonists when Brooke delivered their crisp salads. They were deliciously bright and fresh.

"That salad was almost good enough to make me take up gardening," Cass said when Brooke walked back over to collect their empty plates. "But I don't have a green thumb."

Brooke smiled. "I'm afraid the salad wouldn't have existed if they counted on me to grow greens. We have fantastic gardeners here."

The entrée turned out to be equally fresh, as it was locally caught striped bass fillets, cooked simply and to perfection, and Faith and Cass ate every bite.

When they were done, Cass patted her stomach. "I am pleasantly stuffed. I may have to take a nap instead of writing this afternoon."

"It was delicious. The meals here have ruined me for my own cooking." Faith was a little disappointed that Wolfe hadn't joined them for lunch, but she knew he must be busy. "Is there anything else you would like to see?"

Cass shook her head. "I'm going to walk off some of this wonderful lunch in the gardens. Do you have any greenhouses? I have a great scene in mind that takes place in a greenhouse."

"We have several," Faith said. She gave Cass directions through the gardens. "It's a bit of a walk, but the gardens are lovely and I think you'll find it's worth it."

Brooke rushed over as they set their napkins on the table. "Are you ready for dessert? We have fresh fruit salad, and we just finished a batch of Devonshire cream."

Cass and Faith held up their hands and groaned in unison.

"I'm sure it's delightful," Cass said, "but I can't eat another bite."

"I could wrap one up for you, if you want to take it to your room," Brooke suggested. "In case you need a midafternoon pick-me-up."

"No thank you," Cass said. "By the time I'm hungry again, it'll be dinner. I can definitely say that no one starves in this place."

Brooke beamed in response before turning to Faith. "Do you want me to wrap one up for you?"

Before Faith could answer, the bustle of the kitchen fell silent. The sudden cessation of sound was as startling as a shout.

Faith turned to see Marlene storming toward them.

Marlene pointed at Faith. "Return to the library immediately. Your cat has lost his mind."

17

When Faith reached the doors to the library, she found Watson sitting on the other side of the glass, yowling, while several guests peered at him from the gallery side. Pulling the keys out of her purse, Faith politely excused herself as she moved through the small crowd.

As soon as she opened the door, Watson shot through the crack and raced down the gallery before Faith could catch him.

Great. I hope Marlene doesn't spot him. "I'm sorry about the noise," she told the group. "My cat isn't usually so disruptive."

Mildred, the elderly guest with the fondness for pink trench coats and fedoras, patted Faith's arm. The little Maltese she held was still wearing its matching pink fedora. "I don't think it was his fault. Rupert had his poodle here earlier, and the dog was barking at your cat through the door. I'm sure that's what upset your kitty."

"That poodle is a menace," a pinch-faced woman added. "This morning it chewed up my best fedora. My hat blew off during the garden tour, and that wretched beast jumped on it."

"It still doesn't excuse Watson," Faith said, though she suspected they were right about what set him off. Watson enjoyed teasing the dogs sometimes. She smiled at each of them. "And I'm sorry I kept you waiting. Do you want to check out a book?"

"Not at the moment. I just came to browse," the pinch-faced woman said, then strolled over to the noir display.

"I'm bringing one back," Mildred said, holding up a Raymond Chandler novel. "I could reread *The Big Sleep* a hundred times and get something new from it every time."

"I feel the same way about my favorite books," Faith said.

Mildred peered at Faith shrewdly. "I heard you're the one who found Benjamin. What do you think is going on around here?"

"Going on?" Faith repeated.

"Someone's bumping off private eye enthusiasts," Mildred replied. "I know Oscar North loved the genre too. I remember seeing him at past events."

"I heard he wasn't well-liked," Faith said. "And that he had a history with Benjamin."

"You mean that awful prank." Mildred hugged her tiny dog. "I'll never understand practical jokes. Exactly what is amusing about cruelty?"

Faith didn't have an answer to that. "So you've been coming to So Noir events for a long time?"

Mildred nodded. "Since the group formed. My late husband and I joined at the beginning. I can recapture a little of our fun together when I come."

"Do you know any of the other members who were at the event where the prank happened?" Faith asked.

"Nina maybe, though I think she might have come on later. She's such a fixture now that it's hard to remember. She's been wild about Benjamin since the first time she laid eyes on him." Mildred smiled. "There's no accounting for taste, but then I suppose that's true of us all."

"I suppose," Faith said. "Nina was certainly upset about that trick."

"That's not surprising. It was a mean one."

"Do you know if any of the regulars are members of any fraternities?"

The older woman laughed. "I just put on a trench coat and hat and attend. I don't poke into people's lives. No one has ever mentioned any fraternity to me."

"I ask because my cat found a fraternity pin on the balcony."

"Those are pretty small, right?" She reached up and tapped the corner of her glasses. "With my vision, I wouldn't know if someone wore a dozen little pins. Do you think it had something to do with the murder? I imagine a lot of people step out on that balcony. I did it myself. The view is lovely."

"That's a good point."

Another guest walked up to ask Faith a question about collecting noir novels, and she watched as Mildred and her little dog drifted away.

Eventually the crowd thinned again, and Faith took out her phone to examine the photos Louellyn had sent. They were too small to make out any details, so she e-mailed the pictures to herself and headed for her desk to examine them on her laptop.

She was crossing the room when she spotted movement on the spiral staircase. She looked up to see Watson peering down at her. "I'm glad you're back," she said. "I hope you haven't gotten into any trouble. I suspect Marlene isn't done scolding me for your last episode."

Watson hunched, the muscles of his back and legs rippling under his black-and-white coat, and leaped from the step, landing lightly on one of the bookshelves. From there the cat jumped to the back of one of the armchairs, then to the floor. He trotted over to Faith and dropped something pale at her feet.

"What do you have now?" She bent over and picked up the tiny round object. It was a button, an exact match to the button Benjamin had clutched in his hand. "Where did you get this?"

Watson's only response was to rub against her ankles, clearly pleased with himself.

Since the library was almost empty and no one needed her assistance at the moment, Faith carried the button over to her desk and sat down to see what she could learn about the fraternity behind the pin and buttons. She wasn't sure what help that would give her, but it felt like a step in the right direction. First she opened the photos from Louellyn and looked over the pins in the collection. It was soon obvious that wasn't going to be much help. The photos combined bad lighting and fuzzy focus, so she could tell almost nothing from them.

With a sigh, Faith turned instead to the website her aunt had sent. On it, the emblems for the various fraternities were much clearer, but she quickly realized that clear photos didn't help much when there were so many. She held the button up beside the screen and squinted as she studied the fraternity pins on display.

Her concentration on the photos was so intense that the room around her virtually disappeared. Watson hopped up onto the desk and joined her in peering at the screen, and she hardly noticed him.

A firm hand rested on her shoulder, and Faith shrieked, leaping to her feet. She spun to find Wolfe standing there.

Amusement and chagrin seemed to battle on his face. "I'm sorry. I didn't mean to scare you." He glanced down at the computer. "What had you so focused?"

Faith pressed a hand to her chest, feeling the pounding of her heart through her palm. "I was checking out a site my aunt sent me. It's for collectors of fraternity pins, and I was trying to find a match for the pin Watson found." She held out her other hand. The button lay in her palm. "Watson brought this to me today. I think it's the same one Benjamin was clutching."

Wolfe took the button from her palm and studied it. "It is the same."

"Now if we only knew what fraternity that is."

"Actually, I do. I spoke with Chief Garris this morning." He handed back the button. "It's a professional fraternity. A business fraternity. It's coed, as many professional fraternities are. So both the pin and the buttons could have come from a man or a woman."

Faith set the button beside her computer. "That doesn't narrow down the suspect pool much. In fact, knowing it could have been a woman only makes identifying the killer more difficult." She remembered Nina telling her that she was a business executive in her "real" life. Was she also a member of the fraternity?

"Perhaps," Wolfe said, pulling her out of her musing. "But we don't need to find the murderer. That's the job of the police." He scratched

Watson behind the ears, and the cat closed his eyes and purred loudly. "I'm sorry I missed lunch. Did Cass enjoy seeing the basement?"

"She was disappointed. She hoped it would be dark and spooky."

Wolfe chuckled. "That wouldn't improve employee morale much considering how many people work down there. Plus, I don't really want anyone preparing our meals in the dark."

"Me neither," Faith said. "Cass did enjoy the lunch. The fish couldn't have been fresher."

"We buy from local fishermen as much as possible," Wolfe said, giving Watson one last pat.

With the petting over, Watson stood up to stretch, then jumped down to the floor.

Wolfe nodded toward the cat. "I ran into Marlene on the way here. She said Watson was upsetting the guests."

"Apparently, a poodle barked at him through the locked library door," Faith said with a sigh. "I guess Watson took it as a personal insult because he started yowling. Fortunately, none of the guests seemed upset about it when I got back from lunch."

Wolfe crossed his arms over his chest. "Marlene has tried several times to talk me out of allowing pets onto the property."

Watson meowed mournfully.

They both laughed.

"Don't worry. That will never happen," Wolfe assured the cat, then glanced around the room. "I'm going to be in this evening, and I thought I might do some reading. Since I'm not well-read in noir novels, I could use a recommendation. Which one is your favorite?"

"It's not my preferred genre," Faith said ruefully. "But I have a display over here." She led him to the noir books.

Wolfe picked up one of the novels, scanning the back jacket copy before turning to Faith again. "I have a confession. I stopped by mainly to make sure you were all right. You had a bad shock yesterday."

"We both did. Poor Mr. Mace."

"I might as well admit that I plan to keep an eye on you. If Watson continues bringing you stray clues, you're still potentially in danger."

"I doubt that." She waved a hand around the room. "What can be safer than a library?"

He nodded. "But I'd rather you didn't walk home alone. If I can't get away to escort you to your cottage, I can send someone down to walk with you."

"That's kind of you, but it's completely unnecessary," Faith said. "I'm fine. I promise. When I close the library today, I'm going out to dinner with Eileen." She considered telling him where they were going but decided against it. It would just get her another lecture about not getting involved—as if she could help it at this point.

"That sounds good." He glanced at the door as a few guests came into the library, and then his gaze returned to Faith. He held up the book. "I'll take this and go, but I will check again later to make sure you're all right." With that, he headed briskly toward the doors leading to the gallery.

Faith turned abruptly to go wait on the guests, only to discover that one had walked over already. She nearly ran into him. "Oh, excuse me," she said.

Preston backed up quickly. He wore one of the ubiquitous trench coats, and it nearly made Faith smile after listening to the man's view on the garments earlier. She noticed that his coat was buttoned up higher than normal, as if he were cold. "No, excuse me. Now I owe you another apology."

"What do you mean?"

"I've been rather aggressive in my defense of Louellyn," Preston confessed. "While I stand behind every word I said, I admit that I can't have been exactly kind to you. Louellyn said you seem determined to find Oscar's murderer, and she appreciates it. And so do I."

"I'm actually not any kind of detective," Faith said. "I'm not qualified to track down killers. We have a very good police force for that."

"And I'm going to trust that they will do their job well." Preston smiled tightly. "After all, there isn't much choice beyond trust." He hesitated for a moment before continuing. "I have a question to ask you."

"Yes?"

"I realized that such a fantastic book collection might contain a book I've been trying to find. It's out of print, having had only a few small print runs many years ago."

"What book is that?" she asked.

He rattled off a title that Faith recognized immediately. She looked at him in surprise. "Are you interested in local history?"

"I'm doing a little genealogy project," he said. "While I was researching family connections, I found a reference to the book. I think it may have some information about my grandfather. He was a bit of a rascal."

"Well, I happen to know we do have a copy." She guided him over to one of the tall bookcases that held the books related to New England. Many were out of print, but none were first editions or valuable enough to end up in one of the protected display cases. She reached up for the book, only to realize she was too short. Then she remembered she'd used the library ladder the last time she'd retrieved books from that shelf. "Just a moment. Let me get the ladder."

"Don't bother," Preston said. "I believe I can get it." As he reached up for the shelf, his coat pulled back, revealing a torn cuff on his shirt sleeve. The cuff button was missing.

A chill crept up her spine as Faith stared at the torn cuff. Was that where Watson got the button he'd brought to her? "You've torn your shirt," she said casually, scanning the library to be certain they weren't alone.

The man glanced down at the exposed cuff. "Yes, I caught it on a trellis this morning during the garden tour. I put on the coat to hide the tear once I came in so I didn't have to change. It's an old shirt but a comfortable one." He smiled slightly. "If Louellyn saw it, she'd scold me. She's always telling me I dress like a hobo."

"I know the air-conditioning is rather chilly in here, but aren't you awfully warm in a coat?" Faith asked.

"Not really. I get cold easily." Preston returned to the shelf and grabbed the book. "If you don't mind, I think I'll sit next to the fireplace and spend some time hunting for mention of my grandfather." He chuckled. "I hope I don't discover anything too scandalous, but I suppose we all have skeletons in our family closets."

"I suppose," Faith said. She watched the man carry the book to the fireplace and wondered how she could find out if he was in a business fraternity. He was Oscar's business partner, so the fraternity seemed like a good fit.

Watson walked over to Faith and stared fixedly toward the fireplace. Faith noticed the cat's stump of a tail flipping back and forth in agitation. Then the cat sneezed several times.

She bent and scooped up Watson. "You don't like him much, do you?" she whispered.

Watson wiggled until Faith put him down. She expected him to settle on a chair somewhere, but instead he took advantage of the open door to dash out into the gallery.

Faith groaned. She didn't want Watson running around the manor when Marlene was already annoyed with him.

Since Preston seemed comfortable and no one else was trying to get her attention, she left the library to search for Watson. At first she couldn't find the cat in the vast two-story gallery. "Watson!" she called as she walked farther from the library.

Then she spotted a black-and-white blur heading through an open door used only by staff to access a small, discreet hallway.

Faith frowned, wondering why someone had left the door open, especially with a manor full of wannabe private investigators. She followed Watson and hoped to catch him before he was too far into the staff areas. *It's like he's looking for Marlene so I can get yelled at.*

When she reached the doorway, she saw Watson glaring at a man

Faith didn't recognize, though he wore the normal dark pants and white shirt that set him apart as staff.

The man was squatting and holding out a bit of food toward Watson, but the cat clearly wasn't interested. Instead, Watson was stiff-legged and his fur stood on end.

"Come on, kitty," the man growled. "Just come here, you nuisance."

"Don't touch my cat!" Faith shouted.

The stranger's head whipped around, and he gaped at her. Then he jumped up and ran.

The movement was so familiar that Faith knew instantly that it was the man who'd taken her purse.

He didn't get far before Watson used his skills at tripping once again. This time the cat managed to leap clear before the man could land on him.

With the man sprawled on the floor, Faith took a deep breath and yelled for help at the top of her lungs.

18

Several employees rushed to Faith's aid in response to her shout. It turned out the strange man wasn't employed by Castleton at all, and the police were called.

Officer Tobin grinned when he saw the culprit. "Watson does it again! This guy works for Michael Burke."

"I recognized the way he moved when he started to run," Faith said. "I'm sure he's the man who stole my purse. He was limping when he fled that night. I wonder if there's still some sign of that on him."

"Good question." Officer Tobin walked over and hauled the man's pant leg up, revealing a bruised shin. "Isn't that interesting? Maybe you want to tell us what's going on, Tony. It might go better for you if you do."

"I don't know what you're talking about," the man snarled.

"But why would he want to take Watson?" Faith asked.

Officer Tobin kicked the man's foot lightly. "What do you say? Why were you after the cat? Did Burke send you to grab him?"

The man crossed his arms and glared for a moment, then shook his head. "The boss fired me because I didn't get the blackbird chip. I thought maybe bringing him the cat would get me back in his good graces. He could use the cat to make her turn over the chip."

"I don't have it," Faith said. "I gave it to the police. I told Burke that."

The purse snatcher slumped. "He didn't tell me."

"It's okay, Tony," Officer Tobin said. "I bet there's all kinds of things we can talk about down at the station."

If the man had a response, he didn't give it.

"Snagging Tony Mabin might just give us the leverage we need." Officer Tobin reached out to pat the cat on the head. "You're one top cop, Watson."

The cat purred loudly in response.

Finally, Faith pulled into the parking lot of Driftwood, snagging the spot right beside her aunt's ruby-red Mustang. As she stepped out of her SUV, the hot, humid air hit her like a soggy pillow. Usually evening brought cooler, lighter air, especially so close to the water, but tonight the weather seemed determined to remind Faith of the most unpleasant aspects of summer. She lifted her thick hair off the back of her neck in case a breeze wanted to cool her skin. It didn't.

We're definitely not eating on the deck tonight, she thought as she climbed the wide steps to the restaurant door. She found her aunt waiting on one of the long benches near the hostess stand.

Eileen popped up as soon as she saw Faith and gave her a hug.

"I called for reservations," Faith said. "You shouldn't have had to wait."

"I was in no hurry. They're clearing our table now." Eileen regarded Faith carefully. "You look tired and stressed. I can tell this horrible business at the manor is wearing you down." She shook a finger at Faith. "You need to be careful that you don't make yourself sick."

Faith smiled. "It seems to be my day for getting warnings. Wolfe practically insisted I have a guard walk me back to the cottage today."

"Good for him." Then Eileen's eyes twinkled. "Though it would be nice if he took the job himself. He'd make a nice bodyguard."

Faith nudged her aunt. "You are incorrigible. He's my boss and my friend. It doesn't need to be more than that." She pointedly changed the subject. "I did have something good happen. Well, sort of."

Eileen tugged her over to the bench to sit. "Tell me all about it."

"The police caught the man who stole my purse." She related the incident. "Officer Tobin seemed to think this would be a big help in their case against Michael Burke."

"Are they going to arrest Burke?" Eileen asked.

"It seemed like it was imminent."

Before she could say more, the hostess called Faith's name, and they rose to follow her to the table.

Once they were seated and alone at the table, Eileen perused her menu and asked, "Anything else interesting happen today? You seem to be packing your days lately."

Faith smiled. "I had a lovely lunch with Cass Morton, and Watson brought me a shirt button with the same fraternity symbol on it as the button in Benjamin Mace's hand. It's been a mixed day."

"You wanted to come here so you could talk to Louellyn." Eileen raised her eyebrows. "So is this dinner a continuation of the investigation?"

"That was the original plan," Faith answered. "I wanted to ask her if I could see Oscar's fraternity pin collection in person. The photos she sent me were terrible."

"Why has the plan changed?"

"Wolfe told me the police have identified the fraternity pin and button that Watson found. They're from a coed business fraternity. So that opens the suspect pool to everyone basically, but it does mean I don't need to stare at any more fraternity pins on that website."

Eileen cringed. "It *was* awful. I had a headache in the first five minutes."

"I'm sorry about that."

A young woman in the restaurant's uniform made her way between the tables to stand beside them. "Can I get you something to drink while you look over the menu?"

"I already know what I want," Eileen said. "I'm just going to have a salad. I need more greens in my life."

"Actually that sounds wonderful," Faith agreed.

Eileen ordered the chef's specialty salad with seared tuna and mixed greens, and Faith ordered a Cobb salad. They both chose iced tea, and the waitress gathered their menus and hurried away to get their drinks.

Faith noticed Eileen rubbing her hands and asked, "Are your hands bothering you?"

"Only a little. It's the humidity." She smiled brightly at Faith. "I'll do some knitting when I get home. It helps work out the ache."

Faith nodded, but she still felt bad. Eileen was one of the kindest people she knew. It didn't seem fair that she had to suffer from rheumatoid arthritis. Of course, as her mother had told her many times when she was growing up, *Life isn't fair, but it is interesting.*

"How well do you know Preston Barnwell?" Faith asked, remembering the curious encounter she'd had with the man.

"Not very well," Eileen said. "He isn't a very easy man to get to know. He seems like a quiet sort but clearly devoted to Louellyn and Oscar."

"I certainly believe he's devoted to Louellyn," Faith said. "But he didn't think Oscar treated her right, especially about money. And I agree with your earlier assessment of him. I think he's in love with her."

"That much was obvious every time I saw them together. It must have complicated the partnership," Eileen observed. "I wonder if Oscar knew."

"I don't know, but I saw Preston's shirt cuff today. He was missing a button. He also had a bandage on his arm the day after Oscar died. And he limped the day after my purse was stolen."

Eileen gave Faith a dubious expression. "But you know he's not the thief."

"True, but he could have hurt his leg in an attack on Oscar."

"Or all of those things could be some sort of coincidence."

"I suppose." Faith paused as the waitress showed up with their iced tea, promising the salads would be out soon. Faith took a long sip from the tall glass and found the tea was perfectly made, neither too sweet nor too strong. "It's delicious."

"Everything here is." Eileen drooped in her seat. "It's all so sad. This is a flourishing business. If Oscar hadn't gotten involved with gambling, they would most likely be doing just fine. If you ask me, I think the gambling is the root of everything."

"But I don't see how Burke could have anything to do with Benjamin Mace. And I don't know where the fraternity comes in."

"There's nothing that says a mobster can't belong to a business fraternity, especially if his legal front is business."

Faith chuckled. "I don't know that he's a mobster, though he's definitely a criminal. He admitted that much to me."

Eileen shivered. "It's frightening that you had any contact with that man. Mobsters, illicit relationships—this is all too much like a noir novel. And I find I don't like that kind of story nearly as well when my niece is right in the middle of one."

"I'll be fine." Then Faith raised her glass and grinned. "'You're a good man, sister.'"

Eileen rolled her eyes at the quote from *The Maltese Falcon*.

The salads showed up then, and they turned to more pleasant talk over the light, fresh meal. Eileen told Faith a funny story about a little boy at the library, triggering amusing anecdotes of children they'd known. The time passed quickly, and Faith found she felt much better by the time she forked up the last bite of greens.

"Eileen! Faith! You two are always sneaking in here."

They both turned to see Louellyn winding her way through the tables toward them. Eileen and Faith rose as she approached.

Louellyn hugged Eileen. Then she smiled and scolded her some more. "You should tell me when you're coming so I can do something special."

"Everything Driftwood makes is special," Eileen told her. "And you have more than enough to think about these days."

The smile faded from Louellyn's face. "Mostly I find I'm trying not to think of it. May I join you for a few minutes? It would be nice to talk with friends who don't expect too many smiles."

"Of course." Eileen gestured toward the spare chair, and they all sat down.

"The Cobb salad really hit the spot," Faith said. "To be honest, I'm surprised you're open. Things are hard enough for you right now without having to worry about running a business."

"You'd think that, but honestly, it helps to stay busy. I've hired our fill-in chef to work full-time, which he seems to be enjoying. We're lucky to have him. Is it terrible if I say it's restful to have a kitchen free of drama? Oscar was a brilliant chef, but he could be temperamental about food."

"An artistic trait," Eileen remarked.

Louellyn shrugged. "I guess so. But this chef is so much more open about ingredients, which Oscar treated like state secrets. That drove the servers crazy because sometimes guests had allergy-related questions."

"Allergies are tricky," Faith said. "I know Castleton always asks guests extensively about food allergies, because they're so dangerous. In fact, Brooke had to cleanse the kitchen of strawberries this week because a guest had an undisclosed allergy."

"That would have thrown Oscar into a full-on temper tantrum," Louellyn said. "He always seemed to take it as a personal affront whenever anyone had a food allergy. I love that man, but he could be a challenge." Then her eyes suddenly filled. "Not that I wouldn't be happy for another allergy argument if it meant I could talk to him again."

They sat silently for a moment.

Then Faith risked changing the subject slightly. "Thank you for sending those photos of your husband's fraternity pin collection. I learned the pin Watson found came from a business fraternity."

Louellyn's eyes widened. "Really? Oscar had some photos of members of a business fraternity."

"I thought he didn't like the fraternity members," Faith said.

"He didn't. If you're expecting me to make sense of Oscar's behavior, I can't help you. I loved him. I love him still. But there were things about Oscar that I never understood."

Eileen reached over to rest a hand on Louellyn's arm. "Willa Cather once said, 'The heart of another is a dark forest, always, no matter how close it has been to one's own.' I agree. We never truly know ourselves, so how can we truly know someone else?"

Louellyn sighed. "I always thought we had time. But now we don't." She turned to Faith. "As for the photos, I know he didn't like the young men in them. He drew on their faces with a marker."

"Could I see the photos?" Faith asked.

"I could take pictures of them with my phone and send them to you," Louellyn suggested.

Faith remembered the blurry photos of Oscar's pin collection. "Do you think I could come over and see them sometime?"

"You could come tonight if you like. I find I'm not fond of being home alone. So you're certainly welcome to come over. And you too, of course, Eileen. You used to joke about never having seen Oscar's inner sanctum when you visited."

"I do remember he was protective of his home office," Eileen agreed.

Louellyn waved away the thought. "I think that was just his way of keeping me from complaining about the clutter. He kept all his memorabilia in there, and he knew that kind of mess made me crazy. But he said if no one saw it but him, he should be able to have one room to clutter to his heart's content. That seemed fair."

Faith wondered what might be hiding in the clutter of Oscar's office. Did it contain the answer to his murder? "I could come back here when you get off work or meet you at the house. Do you have a specific time in mind?"

"I'm leaving shortly," Louellyn said. "Most of the time I don't have the energy for closing the restaurant. I start feeling Oscar's absence too much here. At least at home, I can imagine he's off in his office. Isn't that silly? At any rate, if you can wait while I finish up, you can both come home with me."

"I'm afraid I can't," Eileen said. "To be honest, my hands are bothering me, and I'd like to go home and take a pain pill. I can't drive once I take one. Besides, my daughter-in-law said she might call. I don't want to miss a chat with the grandkids."

"I'm still game," Faith said, though she felt a small pang of guilt. Going off alone to Louellyn's house almost certainly wouldn't fall within Wolfe's view of being careful. But she didn't think she could pass up this opportunity to get some answers to the question of how the fraternity might connect with the current guests at Castleton.

"I'll go finish up, and then we can leave," Louellyn said, the slightly brittle cheer back in her voice as she stood up. "Your dinner tab is on the house, so don't worry about a check."

"You don't need to do that," Eileen protested, getting to her feet.

Louellyn leaned over and pecked Eileen on the cheek. "What are old friends for? I'm understanding more and more the value of friends. I don't think I'll ever forget now." With that, she turned and walked toward the kitchen.

Eileen sat back down. "Don't let Louellyn keep you out too late. I still don't like how tired you look. And call me when you get home. I'll rest better if I know you're safe."

"Everyone is worried about my safety lately. I'll be fine, but I promise I'll call." Faith took a sip from her glass and turned the conversation to a topic she knew would distract Eileen—her grandchildren. "How are Benjamin and Madison these days? Have they talked their parents into getting goats yet?"

Eileen laughed, her whole face lighting up. "No, the goats were apparently a passing obsession based on a video game. According to Claire, right now they're both totally focused on swimming and entering the Olympics one day."

Faith laughed. "Knowing those two, I wouldn't write them off."

They chatted about family while sipping their drinks, and Faith enjoyed the obvious pleasure on her aunt's face.

By the time they were down to ice and lemon wedges in their glasses, Louellyn came back. "I'm ready to go if you are," she said.

Faith and Eileen stood and gathered their things, then followed Louellyn out to the front of the restaurant.

Eileen gave Faith a quick hug. "Talking about Benjamin and Madison has made me eager to be home for the call." She reached out and squeezed Louellyn's hand. "Please let me know if you need anything."

"I will."

Eileen waved to them as she headed to her car.

Louellyn pointed toward a shadowy far corner of the parking lot. "I'm parked over there. I'll pull up here so you can follow." Then she gave Faith her address. "Just in case we get separated."

"Hopefully I'm good to follow as I don't know this area as well. I'm over there." Faith pointed at her silver Honda.

As Faith followed Louellyn's sporty little car out of the lot, she felt another pang of guilt about not exactly making the safest choice. Once they were on the road, Louellyn's fast driving made it challenging to keep up with her, and Faith had no more time to fret about anything else.

Since Faith wasn't comfortable with speeding on the residential streets, she was soon lagging behind. "Come on, Louellyn," she muttered. "Slow down." She began to worry that she was going to have to pull off and use her phone's GPS to guide her the rest of the way.

She noticed a big truck behind her, matching her turns on the streets. The truck's headlights were on high, and Faith blinked as they flashed in her rearview mirror on the turns. "Tailgating?" she said to the bright image in the mirror. "Are you in such a hurry?"

After glimpsing Louellyn's flash of taillights, Faith turned another corner, but when she looked down the street, she saw no sign of Louellyn. With a groan, she searched for a place to pull over.

The truck behind her crowded up on her tail even more.

"Come on," Faith mumbled. "Just go around me."

Instead, the truck bumped into the back of Faith's SUV.

"What are you doing?" Faith glanced in the rearview mirror.

The truck was close enough now that she could tell it was a dark color. She pressed the gas pedal to put some distance between herself and the erratic driver.

But the truck only picked up speed and bumped her again.

This time, Faith nervously stomped on the gas, increasing the space between her and the driver once more.

The truck rushed up on her, the lights dazzling her in the rearview mirror.

Faith tightened her grip on the steering wheel, bracing for another impact. She knew she was going too fast for these streets. Would another bump make her lose control?

19

Ahead, a car turned onto the street Faith raced down, its headlights flashing in Faith's face. A loud honk made her jump. Obviously the driver coming at her disapproved of her haste.

"So do I," she muttered through gritted teeth.

She risked a glimpse in the rearview mirror. The big dark truck that had rammed her twice was still behind her, but it had fallen back.

Faith took the next turn, struggling to stay in her lane at the speed she was driving. Ahead, she spotted a brightly lit house where a number of cars were parked along the curb. Then she noticed a car slipping into an empty spot. She stomped on her brake to slow enough to make it around all the parked cars.

Anxiously, she glanced in the rearview mirror again. The street behind her was empty. The truck hadn't turned onto the street. Faith continued to slow, gripping the steering wheel so tightly that her knuckles ached. After she'd passed the party house, she pulled over and waited for her heart rate to return to normal.

She picked up her phone from the console. She *should* call the police. There was no question that someone tried to force her off the road, but what could she really tell them about the truck? With the bright lights in her eyes, all she knew was that the truck was big and dark. She hadn't gotten its license plate number. And if she called the police, she'd need to stay right where she was and wait for them. She didn't want to miss seeing Louellyn's photos.

Staring down at the phone in her hand, Faith finally made a decision. She called Brooke and was relieved when her friend answered on the first ring.

"I was just thinking about you. Want to come over for popcorn and a movie?"

"Sounds great," Faith said, her voice shaky. "But I'm on my way to talk to Louellyn North, the widow of the man who fell from the terrace."

"Sleuthing or consoling?" Brooke asked.

"Sleuthing, I guess. I'm going to check out some old photos to see if I recognize any faces. Look, can you do me a favor?" Faith told her friend about the dark truck. "I'm worried that it might have been someone sent by Michael Burke." She went on to catch Brooke up on the arrest of the purse snatcher.

Brooke gasped. "That's crazy. Do you want me to come meet you?"

"No, I just wanted someone else to know what had happened and that I was at Louellyn's. I'll call you back as soon as I finish at her house," Faith said. "But would you consider going over to the cottage and taking Watson home with you until you hear from me? I'm not comfortable leaving him alone. Burke already sent someone to my house once. Since running me off the road didn't work, I'm worried that he might go to my house again."

"Sure," Brooke said. "But I don't like this."

"It'll be fine. Perhaps you shouldn't go to the cottage alone, though. Maybe you could get Midge to come with you. I know I'm being a bit paranoid, but I am a little scared for Watson."

"You are being cautious, but in this case I think it's justified," Brooke assured her. "You need to call the police."

"Maybe I will but not until after this meeting with Louellyn. I'd appreciate it if you'd call the police if you don't hear back from me in an hour. Tell them where I am." Faith rattled off Louellyn's address.

"I can do that, but I don't like this at all. You need someone there with you," Brooke insisted.

"Louellyn will be with me. I'm a little rattled, but I'm fine. Just wait to hear from me, okay?"

"Okay," Brooke said. "I'll call Midge and head to your cottage right now. But I'm calling the police if you're even one second late getting in touch with me."

"I'm counting on it." After Faith ended the call, she brought up the GPS app and scanned the route to Louellyn's. She was a few blocks away, but she was no longer shaking so she felt safe driving again.

She found Louellyn standing in the driveway of a large Victorian. The relief on the woman's face was obvious.

As soon as Faith pulled in, Louellyn rushed to her door. "I was so worried. I know I was driving too fast, and I'm sorry. When I realized I'd lost you, I tried to call but I couldn't get through."

When she stepped back, Faith eased the door open. "I called a friend to go check on Watson. He hates being left alone." She couldn't give Louellyn more to worry about. Still, she felt a twinge of guilt at the unspoken truth. The smile she offered Louellyn felt tight. "I'm sorry I worried you."

Louellyn flapped a hand. "It's not your fault. I'm the one who raced off and lost you. I seem to be worrying all the time lately. I've been driving Preston crazy." She started to walk up the driveway to the house.

Faith fell into step beside her. "He seems to be someone you can rely on," she said carefully.

"He's been a rock," Louellyn responded. "But with everything he's going through, I feel guilty leaning on him."

"Everything he's going through?" Faith repeated.

They'd reached the door, and Louellyn opened it and ushered Faith inside. "He's sick. It's an autoimmune disorder with some awful name. I couldn't tell you what, but I think the medication he takes is almost as bad as the symptoms of the disease. One of the meds he's on causes his skin to split sometimes. Can you imagine? The poor man is always covered in bandages or limping."

"That sounds terrible."

Louellyn nodded. Then she glanced around the foyer where they stood as if trying to make a plan. "Do you want a cup of coffee or something before we go snooping?"

"That sounds nice, but I don't want to stay too late. I have another stop to make before I go home, and I've never been much of a night owl."

"And here I am, nattering about Preston."

"It's not a problem. I've talked to him a few times at the manor." Faith hesitated, then decided to broach a delicate subject. "I'm fairly certain he has feelings for you."

Louellyn groaned softly. "Yes, I know. I've always known, but Preston's been good about not acting inappropriately, so I guess we both pretend those feelings don't exist. I think he knows I don't share them. Oscar was the love of my life. Still is."

"Do you think that will ever change?" Faith asked.

"I can't see the future, but if someday I feel ready to consider dating, it won't be Preston. He doesn't have that much time left. He's dying."

"I'm so sorry to hear that."

"I'll be the best friend I can be while he needs me, but that's all I have to offer." Louellyn slumped a little and turned to lead Faith down a hallway. "Preston understands that. He and Oscar were old friends, and I know all this has hit him hard too. Honestly, I worry about whether Preston is eating. And the way he's been dressing since the accident. The man is practically wearing rags. He says they're comfortable on his sore skin." She paused in front of a heavy oak door. "Okay, prepare to enter the inner sanctum."

She opened the door, and they walked into a large, cluttered office. The walls had dark paneling, and the light Louellyn switched on did little to chase away the shadows in the corners of the room. Faith could see Oscar had favored heavy, dark furniture.

"The photos are with the pin collection." Louellyn went over to a built-in floor-to-ceiling bookcase that took up one entire wall. She reached up and pulled down a cardboard box, then turned and set it on a dark leather chair, one of the few surfaces not already piled with things. "You know, I can't face the thought of cleaning out this room. I may just shut the door for a year. Do you think that makes me a coward?"

Faith smiled at her. "I'd say it makes you human. It's completely reasonable to want to wait until the grief isn't so fresh."

Louellyn opened the box and took out a smaller box. The fraternity pins were simply thrown into it haphazardly.

"You went to a lot of trouble to lay these out for the photograph," Faith said, suddenly feeling bad about her grumpy thoughts regarding the blurry photos. "Thank you."

"It was no trouble. Busywork suits me at the moment. That's how Oscar stored them, so I guess it was a bit of a stretch to call it a collection."

Faith started examining the pins.

Louellyn turned back to the larger box and removed a small, worn photo album. "This contains the pictures I mentioned. I asked Oscar once why he kept albums from all his old jobs. He said when he was a world-famous chef, he'd need photos from his early days for publicity. But it doesn't explain why he wrote on some of them." As she handed over the thin album, her face became sad. "Now that I think of it, I guess these are just records of a man who never quite fulfilled his dream."

"I don't know about that," Faith said. "He had a successful business, a wife who loved him, and real talent. I think he fulfilled a lot of dreams."

Louellyn's expression lifted slightly. "Maybe."

Faith opened the album. The first page showed a group of young men mugging for the camera with cheesy grins and arms slung over each other's shoulders. As Louellyn had said, the photo was badly disfigured. Although Faith could pick out Oscar, young and mildly unhappy, the other faces sported ink mustaches and glasses, and one even had a pair of devil horns and a thick *X* across it.

Faith studied that face in particular, trying to see past the ink and imagine what the passage of time might have done to the grinning young man. Something about him seemed familiar. She put her finger over the *X* so that just the young man's eyes showed. She gasped. Without the distraction of the ink, she recognized those eyes. Stunned, she stared at the photo album in her hands.

Then Louellyn spoke up. "Do you smell smoke?"

20

Faith's distraction over the man in the photo had kept the smell from registering in her brain, but when Louellyn pulled her attention away, Faith noticed the sharp scent of smoke hanging in the air.

"That's weird," Louellyn said as she walked toward the door. "The smoke alarms should have gone off."

Faith rushed over before Louellyn could put her hand on the doorknob. "Wait." She pointed at the smoke coming in under the door. "Smoke rises, so if it's visibly coming under the door, that's a really bad sign." She put her hand against the wood and felt the warmth that was a stark contrast to the cool, air-conditioned room. "We'd better not open that door."

"It's the only door."

Faith whirled to look around the room. A single window behind the desk was partially blocked by a table piled high with books and boxes. "We can go out the window. Help me move the table."

They dragged the table out of the way.

Faith coughed as the smoky air burned the back of her throat. She unlocked the window and pulled on it. It was stuck.

Louellyn took up a spot beside her, and they tugged on the window together. But it still didn't budge. Finally, they stopped, the combination of smoke and exertion making them cough harder.

Faith peered closely at the window. "I think it's painted shut. Did Oscar have scissors or anything sharp in his desk?"

"Maybe."

They rifled through the desk until Louellyn found a letter opener and Faith located a small pair of scissors. They used the blades to gouge around the window. Faith winced at what she was doing to the paint, but with the smoke becoming more obvious in the room, she doubted that chipped paint was the worst damage the house suffered that night. At last they yanked on the window, and it opened.

Clutching the photo album with what she was certain was a picture of the killer, Faith scrambled through the window, landing in a hedge outside. She dropped the album onto the ground and ignored the sharp scratches from the bush as she helped Louellyn squirm out the window.

When they were both safely outside, Faith heard someone calling Louellyn's name.

"Mrs. Witlow?" Louellyn yelled back.

An elegantly dressed older woman made a beeline to them from the front of the house. "Thank heavens. I was so frightened for you when I saw the smoke. Are you all right, dear? I've called 911."

"Thank you," Louellyn said. "I appreciate your help."

"Did you see anyone else over here?" Faith asked. "A man maybe?"

The older woman shook her head. Then her eyes widened in alarm. "Preston isn't in there, is he?"

Louellyn caught the woman's hands. "No, we were alone."

Alone except for whoever set the fire. Faith retrieved the album from the ground and hugged it.

Louellyn was still talking to her neighbor. "You should go on home now. The firemen will be here shortly, and all we can do is hope they can save the house."

"You should come with me," Mrs. Witlow said. "I'll make coffee."

"That sounds nice. You go on ahead. Faith and I will be there in a minute." Louellyn turned to Faith. "Maybe we should move our cars. I would imagine the fire trucks need to be near the house."

Still numb from the revelation in the photo album and the house fire, Faith merely nodded.

As they walked toward the cars, Louellyn stumbled.

Faith reached out to hold her arm. "Are you all right?"

Louellyn nodded, but Faith could feel her shaking. "It's just too much. Oscar. My home." She blinked as she gazed at the house.

"At least we made it out."

"You sound like Eileen, finding the bright spot in a dark situation." Louellyn shivered. "Do you think you could move the cars and wait for the fire trucks? I know it's a lot to ask, but I would really like to take Mrs. Witlow up on that coffee."

"Of course. I can move the cars."

"My keys are in the console." Louellyn smiled shakily. "Oscar used to scold me for leaving my keys in the car and leaving it unlocked at home, but I was always hunting for them otherwise." She seemed to realize she was babbling and put a hand up to her mouth.

"It'll be fine," Faith soothed. "You go on ahead."

Louellyn turned toward the neighbor's house and disappeared.

Faith wondered if she should follow her to make sure she got there safely. The fire had been set by someone, and that person was probably out to get Louellyn. There was no guarantee the arsonist and murderer wasn't still lurking in the darkness.

Then someone emerged from the shadows. Even before the person walked into the limited light, Faith could tell it was a man by the broad shoulders.

Faith took a step back. "The police are on their way," she announced.

The man walked into the light. Jordan Pointe smirked at her and raised the gun in his hand. "Then I shouldn't dillydally." He gestured with the gun at the photo album in Faith's hands. "I assume that contains some kind of evidence, since you took the time to carry it out of a burning house. You'd best give it to me."

Faith stood perfectly still. "The police will figure it out even without the album. They have identified your fraternity, and they know the killer is a guest at the manor. How many of the guests are likely to share your same fraternity affiliation?"

He smiled. "It might surprise you. Now hand over the album."

Faith still didn't move. "None of this makes sense. What did Oscar ever do to you?"

"He ruined my life," the man snarled. With rage distorting his features, Faith wondered how she could ever have thought him handsome.

"Ruined your life? Don't you have your own business? You certainly don't look ruined."

"Do you have any idea how long it's taken me to get where I am, all because of Oscar? You see, my father owned one of the finest restaurants in Boston, and Oscar wanted in. But I wasn't there to be some footstool for the help, and I told him so."

Well, that explains the art on the photo. "That sounds more like a reason Oscar would be mad at you, not the other way around."

"Except that Oscar always had to win. Always. He knew I had an allergy to strawberries. He knew all the allergies. After all, it was his job to keep our food safe. But somehow strawberry puree accidentally got into my birthday cake instead of the raspberry that it was supposed to be."

"And you got sick," Faith said.

"Sick? My face swelled up in lumps. My eyes swelled shut. I was hideous, and everyone saw it. The guys called me Lumpy for months. I laughed along with them, but my girlfriend didn't think it was amusing. She had a social standing to consider."

"You murdered Oscar because your college girlfriend was shallow?" Faith said.

"My girlfriend was the daughter of one of the richest men in the country. I was going to marry into that family. My future was guaranteed. I wouldn't have been clawing and scraping to make my way to owning a lousy bookstore."

"You killed Oscar because you had to work for a living?"

"I didn't *kill* Oscar," the bookseller insisted. "I saw him on the first night of the retreat. He was upstairs looking for a guest's room. He stopped me in the hall and asked me if I knew someone named

Preston. He didn't know who I was. He stole my future, and he didn't even recognize me."

"It has been many years," Faith said.

Jordan continued talking as if he hadn't heard her, and perhaps he hadn't. "I confronted him. I was going to see that recognition in his face and then belt him. When I finally got through, I saw it. He knew me. He laughed and called me Lumpy. I took a swing at him. I was so angry I probably would have knocked his head off if the punch had landed, but Oscar ducked, then ran. I went after him, but he was fast. He was up on the balcony rail before I could reach him. He was clearly planning to jump, but I made a grab for him. I wanted to pull him back and land that punch. But he went over the rail. It wasn't my fault. It was an accident, not murder."

Faith had a hard time believing his story. "And Benjamin Mace? What did he accidentally fall from?"

"He got what he deserved for not leaving things alone," he scoffed. "That man thought he was a detective. He accused me of killing Oscar because I was having an affair with his wife."

Faith gasped. "You were having an affair with Louellyn?" How had she misjudged everything so badly?

"Of course not," Jordan snapped. "I didn't even know her. But Mace had made the connection with the fraternity pin, and if he got the police interested in me, I could get attention I didn't need. So I shut him up. Permanently."

"And you set this fire." Faith waved a hand toward the house. "To get rid of any evidence."

"Evidence and *you*," Jordan growled. "You're as bad as Mace with the meddling. Once you're gone, this whole sordid mess will blow over, and I'll never come to another of these ludicrous noir retreats."

Faith detected movement in the shadows behind Jordan. Had the fire department arrived? "Since you're going to kill me anyway," she said, stalling for time and trying to keep his attention, "I have one last question. What happened to Benjamin Mace's trench coat?"

"I took it. I thought I might need some evidence to plant if things got close to me." He pointed toward the house. "It's in there now, carefully hidden in the fridge. And if the fire department manages to keep it from burning up, it should confuse things nicely, not that you're going to have to worry about it."

Then Faith heard a familiar voice shriek, "Watson, no!"

The killer spun, his gun raised, but he wasn't quick enough. A black-and-white blur landed on his chest and clawed his way to Jordan's face. The man roared and swatted at Watson, dropping his gun in his haste to get rid of the spitting, clawing cat. The gun hit the ground and went off. Jordan groaned and crumpled to the ground, where he clung to his leg in pain.

Watson jumped clear and raced over to Faith.

"Hold it right there!" Officer Tobin shouted, pointing his gun at the bleeding man.

Faith bent to scoop up Watson, hugging him close to her chest.

"You have to help me!" Jordan wailed. "I've been shot."

"An ambulance is on the way," Officer Tobin said as he bent to retrieve the fallen gun. "You're under arrest for the murders of Benjamin Mace and Oscar North. And I'm sure we have a few other charges for you after that detailed confession we just heard."

Brooke joined Faith, with Wolfe close behind her.

"What are you doing here?" Faith asked Brooke.

"I couldn't wait," Brooke said. "Watson was meowing and pacing when I got to your house, and I couldn't calm him down. I knew something was wrong, so I called Wolfe and rushed over here."

"And I called the police." Wolfe frowned at Faith. "This is not being careful." Then he sighed. "I'm beginning to get the feeling that *Faith Newberry* and *careful* are words that will never go together."

"I don't go looking for trouble," Faith assured him as she hugged Watson. "It comes to me."

Another case closed. The hard-boiled detective cat accepted the cuddles that were his due. He'd saved his human again. He knew she'd told the truth when she said she never went looking for trouble but trouble found her all the same. As long as that was true, he'd be there to take care of her. After all, when someone goes after a cat's human, he's supposed to do something about it. If a cat lets something bad happen to his human, it's bad all around, bad for every cat everywhere.

The cat tucked his head under his human's chin and purred loud and long in the hot summer night. And with that, nothing more needed to be said.